Cover Copy

He seeks the one his heart desires...

With their fae-blooded clan teetering on the verge of extinction, Jamie Matheson finds himself battling a deep attraction to one of the few remaining unmated women within his clan, a woman he's not permitted to touch unless a soul bond forms between them. Like his fellow clansmen, he must ensure her protection, even if that means from himself.

Annabella wishes to forge a mated bond with only one man, yet when Jamie treks deep into the Highlands in order to put some distance between them, she soon discovers not all is as it seems, not when her very spirit calls out to Jamie's from across the ages. It appears they've both lived in two separate times, here in the future and far in the past, and now if they ever wish to complete the bond and come together as one, they must first right the wrongs of their deadly past. It's time to return to when they first discovered their mated bond began, the year 1211.

Come and immerse yourself in this riveting historical time travel romance, one which crosses the centuries and brings together lost souls.

Books by Joanne Wadsworth

The Matheson Brothers Series
Highlander's Desire, Book One
Highlander's Passion, Book Two
Highlander's Seduction, Book Three
Highlander's Kiss, Book Four
Highlander's Heart, Book Five
Highlander's Sword, Book Six
Highlander's Bride, Book Seven
Highlander's Caress, Book Eight
Highlander's Touch, Book Nine
Highlander's Shifter, Book Ten
Highlander's Claim, Book Eleven
Highlander's Courage, Book Twelve
Highlander's Mermaid, Book Thirteen

Highlander Heat Series
Highlander's Castle, Book One
Highlander's Magic, Book Two
Highlander's Charm, Book Three
Highlander's Guardian, Book Four
Highlander's Faerie, Book Five
Highlander's Champion, Book Six
Highlander's Captive (Short Story)

Billionaire Bodyguards Series
Billionaire Bodyguard Attraction, Book One
Billionaire Bodyguard Boss, Book Two
Billionaire Bodyguard Fling, Book Three

Books by Joanne Wadsworth

Regency Brides Series
The Duke's Bride, Book One
The Earl's Bride, Book Two
The Wartime Bride, Book Three
The Earl's Secret Bride, Book Four
The Prince's Bride, Book Five
Her Pirate Prince, Book Six

Princesses of Myth Series
Protector, Book One
Warrior, Book Two
Hunter (Short Story - Included in Warrior, Book Two)
Enchanter, Book Three
Healer, Book Four
Chaser, Book Five

Highlander's Shifter

The Matheson Brothers, Book Ten

JOANNE WADSWORTH

Highlander's Shifter
ISBN-13: 978-1-99-003440-4
Copyright © 2016, Joanne Wadsworth
Cover Art by Joanne Wadsworth
First electronic publication: October 2016

Joanne Wadsworth
http://www.joannewadsworth.com

AUTHOR'S NOTE:
This book is a work of fiction. The names, characters, places, and incidents are products of the writer's imagination or have been used fictitiously and are not to be construed as real. Any resemblance to persons, living or dead, actual events, locale or organizations is entirely coincidental. The author does not have any control over and does not assume any responsibility for third-party websites or their content.

Published in the United States of America

First digital publication: October 2016
First print publication: October 2016

The Fae Village

In the twelfth century, a man named Gilleoin became the first and only known man to hold bear shifter blood, an ability gifted to him by The Most High One. His clan was called Matheson, and when he mated with a woman carrying faerie blood, they created a line shrouded in secrecy, a line guarded by the immortal fae princess, Cherub. Through the endless streams of time, she will be there for them, never forsaking her people, either in the present or far into the past.

The Seer – Nessa

The ancient House of Clan Matheson, led by Gilleoin, the Chief of Clan Matheson, Scotland, 1211.

The midnight hour struck. Filled with dread from a vision, Nessa raced downstairs and halted at the edge of the darkened great hall. The large domed room held a sweeping circlet of wooden beamed rafters rising high overhead with a hundred or so battle-weary warriors sleeping on pallets scattered before the flickering fire. In their black battle leathers and clan plaids, their claymores within arm's reach, her clansmen sought valuable rest following their latest attack from their enemy.

Two of their clan healers quietly moved amongst the men, kneeling before pallets and ensuring wounds were tended and bound. Having had only a mere hour's rest since she'd last aided the healers, she searched amongst the men and found Jamie Matheson, her beloved grandson. He'd been moved closer to the hearth, his disheveled dark hair lying matted with fresh blood to his forehead, the soaked strands gleaming red under the glow of the fire where they poked out from under the cotton wrappings. With his broad shoulders filling out his leather cotun, he clenched his fist around his sword hilt, his knuckles straining white. He held her line's strong fae blood and along with it the "power of thought," his sought-after skill allowing him to move objects or even people with naught but one thought from his mind alone.

Eyes closed and with a slight twitch of his fingers, the wrappings around his head and neck unraveled and plopped to the ground. More blood oozed forth and she staggered to Jamie's side. Her vision had shown her this very moment occurring, one she now dreaded to the depths of her heart.

On her knees, she touched the sides of Jamie's head and neck wound, the stitching no longer keeping the rising swell of blood contained. Gently, she scooped Jamie's head from the pillow and cradled it in her lap. "Dinnae allow the deep sleep yet, my dear."

"Grandmother." Sluggishly, he opened his eyes and with a dazed gaze murmured under his breath, "T-there is naught to be done to heal me. I can sense it. W-when Annabella returns from the v-village, tell her I"—more blood, and far too much—"I-love her."

"You must hold on so you might tell her yourself." Within her vision, she'd seen Jamie's death, yet she'd also seen what was to come for him. In a time so far from her own, he'd be reborn and his spirit would live on. Even as grief assailed her, the knowledge of his rebirth brought her at least a little peace.

"You've seen my death. That's w-why you're here." His dazed gaze cleared a touch. "Tell me all."

"Even though I didnae wish for you to leave us, I've seen that an even greater future awaits you in another time. Your spirit will live on and be reborn almost eight-hundred years from now. Far in the future, you will stand at Murdock Matheson's side, the seer and chief of our twenty-first century clan. Gilleoin no longer needs you, but Murdock surely does."

"Then I shall go to Murdock." He shuddered in her arms. "T-tell Annabella to come to me t-there. Wherever I lead, she follows."

"I shall, my dear."

His eyes slid shut, his hand sliding limply from his sword and flopping onto the pallet. A gentle, heavenly white glow swirled from his chest, wisped around her and whooshed through the open window.

Sobs wracked through her and she slumped over Jamie's chest and rocked. Clutching him to her, she wept until she could weep no more.

For hours, she remained that way, pushing away the comforting hands of the healers as they tried to soothe her and instead she bid them to leave her be.

Only as the sun rose and a new day dawned did she finally rise and stagger into the side antechamber where their chief, Gilleoin, often met with his captains.

Wiping her tears away, she gripped the windowsill and got hit by another vision so hard and fast. Eyes closed, she grappled to pin the rippling images down.

Annabella shimmered forth, Jamie's mate and his soon-to-be bride, or at least she had been. In the dark of the night—this coming night—Annabella stood upon the battlements in a corner where the guards rarely patrolled, her white fur cloak tied tightly around her neck and a heavy mist shrouding her.

Grief stricken, the young lass with the fae empath ability had raced away from her after she'd told her of Jamie's passing and now Annabella braced her hands either side of the crenellation before her and climbed atop it.

On the stony edge, Annabella wobbled, her hands raised to the heavens above and tears streaking down her cheeks. Weeping, she cried out, "Jamie, wait for me, for no matter where you reside beyond the veil, I will find you."

Nay, she couldn't lose Annabella too.

More images hit her, a swirling barrage.

She herself hurried along the misty ramparts toward

Annabella. "Dinnae leave this way," she cried out and managed to snag Annabella's hand as the lass launched herself over the edge. She held on to her kin for dear life as the lass swayed against the curtain wall, naught but the jagged rocks below. "Hold tight to my hand, Annabella."

"Jamie loves me, Nessa, told me to come to him in the twenty-first century where he'll be reborn. Wherever he goes, I go. It has always been that way between us, and right now I wish to join the man I love in death." Annabella jerked her hand from hers and fell.

"Cherub!" Nessa screamed her fae princess's name.

"I'm here." Within the cloying mist, Cherub shimmered in, caught Annabella in her arms and floated upward with her. In her royal blue gown swishing against her legs and her blond hair swaying to her waist, she muttered to the lass, "You should have reached out to me in your time of grief. I would've come."

"Jamie perished this morn in a battle and now I wish to join him." Annabella clung to Cherub, tears spiky and wet on her clumped lashes. "I need to go to him, and it cannae wait any longer."

Nessa clutched her chest. "Cherub, I had a vision moments afore Jamie's death and managed to tell Jamie about it. Annabella as well. That is why she has jumped."

"Tell me about your vision."

"Jamie is destined to live in the future, his spirit reborn almost eight-hundred years from now. He will stand at Murdock Matheson's side, the seer and chief of our twenty-first century clan. He asked that I tell Annabella she's to join him there, and she has chosen that moment as now." The moon broke fully free of darkened clouds overhead and soft moonbeams shimmered through the fog.

"If Jamie is to be reborn in Murdock's time, then by what name will he go by?" Cherub's sparkly skin shimmered in the moon's glow, the enchanting sight denoting her strong royal line.

"I can travel to him through a portal in time and find him, although those who are reborn usually have no prior knowledge of who they were. Still, I can watch over him and ensure he and Annabella find each other again."

"In my vision, I saw that he holds the same name as he does now. Jamie Matheson. Although here he is of fae blood alone, while in the future he holds both fae and shifter blood, through the merging of my daughter's line with Gilleoin's line."

"Good, that information will aid me greatly." To Annabella, Cherub said, "Everything unfolds for a purpose and within its own time, but I shall take you beyond the veil with me first and there you shall remain until the right time arrives for your rebirth to occur. You'll have no prior knowledge of your mated bond with Jamie, but at least in this way I can ensure you dinnae suffer from such a tragic death."

"I'll go anywhere you ask, as long as I get to be with Jamie again." Annabella hugged Cherub tight. "He is my mate, my chosen one, and we've yet to complete the bond. I dearly wish we'd had the chance while he lived. I feel so lost, as if my very soul has been broken in two."

"It isnae good that you missed the chance to complete your bond afore Jamie's death. Your soul and his will never truly be at peace unless I can change your own past and ensure you and Jamie are both given that chance to join as one, although I cannae alter Jamie's death from occurring, no' when he is destined for another faraway time. Neither may you change it either."

Their fae guardian turned her gaze on Nessa. "For me to work a little fae magic to see this done, you must first attend to one very important chore. Connect with your seer ability to Murdock and warn him of what's to come, that he's to keep Jamie and Annabella's rebirth a secret from them until he *sees* the time is right. All must occur at the right time in order for Jamie and Annabella to complete their bond here in the past, and of course far in the future where they will soon reside."

"Provided I never have to watch Annabella fall to her death, then aye, I will do anything you ask of me." She reached over the edge and cupped Annabella's cheek where she bobbed with Cherub. "I love you, as if you were my own granddaughter, and I shall surely miss you in the days and years ahead, just as I already miss Jamie. Travel safely, my dear."

"I'll miss you too." Annabella turned her face into her palm and dropped a kiss there. "Until I see you again, Nessa. One day I will, beyond the veil or in another time."

"Aye, that you shall for we are both of fae blood."

"We must go." Cherub blew her a kiss. "Take care, my friend."

"You too, and thank you for coming so swiftly."

"I shall always come when you or any of my fae-blooded people require my aid." Cherub slowly shimmered, her form disappearing and Annabella's too. Within the blink of an eye, they were gone.

Nessa opened her eyes where she knelt before the window.

Speak to Murdock she would, right now, for this vision she'd had would come into being this very night and she had to pave the way for her grandson and Annabella's rebirth. The future safety of their very hearts and souls might very well depend upon it.

Aye, 'twas just as well she and Murdock could connect through visions with each other, even across the centuries dividing them. He was a seer as she was, and whenever she'd needed his wise counsel, he'd been there for her, just as she'd been there for him.

Eyes closed once more, she waited as more images fluttered at the periphery of her mind. 'Twas Murdock. He stood at his solar window on the second floor of Matheson Castle overlooking the same courtyard as she did, the ancient elm tree near his window swaying in the brisk breeze. She tapped into his mind and whispered across the centuries dividing them, *"I see you, Murdock."*

"As I see you, my friend. I also caught a vision of the moment when you lost your grandson. I'm so sorry for your loss."

"More has occurred since that moment. I've had another vision of Jamie's betrothed, Annabella. She and Jamie have never had the chance to complete their bond, and this night she intends on ending her life. Cherub will come for her, will aid her in her ascension so she need no' suffer a true death, then both she and Jamie will be reborn in your time. Cherub has told me to warn you of what's to come, that you're to keep Jamie and Annabella's rebirth a secret until you 'see' the time is right. Cherub wishes to alter Jamie and Annabella's past, so that they might be able to complete their bond afore Jamie's death occurred this morn. That is the only way to ensure their souls will ever truly be at peace. I ask that you ensure no one tears them apart."

"You have my word I shall guard and watch over them both following their rebirth. Never fear that I won't." A spark of determination flickered in his eyes, likely the same spark which always flickered within hers, for as their clan seers they were devoted to their kin. Each and every one of them, no matter what time they might reside within.

"You have my immense thanks." She touched her heart. *"Until the next time we speak, stay safe."*

"Aye, until the next time."

Murdock's image fluttered away, lost to her through the ages, but not their deep friendship or the knowledge they shared. He'd ensure all remained on course, and so too would Cherub as she watched over her kin.

Chapter 1

Matheson Castle, led by Murdock Matheson, the Chief of Clan Matheson, a man with dual fae-shifter blood, Scotland, current day.

In the darkened side room attached to the interrogation chamber, Jamie Matheson stood hidden behind thick mirrored glass, his hands clasped behind his back and spine stiff as he awaited their head guardsman's arrival with his current case's assailant.

A thrumming reverberated through him, as it always did when one particular member of his clan drew nearer. Annabella, or Bella as she was known to her closest kin and friends. He narrowed his gaze on the door next to him and with only one thought from his mind, kept it held firmly in place.

Ha. See if Bella could get in now.

The door rattled, then stopped, rattled some more then—*thump.*

"Let me in, Jamie." *Thump, thump, thump.* "I know you're in there. Release this door now. I need to speak with you."

"Is there something of dire importance you wished to speak of?" Not a chance was he releasing that door, not when his inner bear was so damn hungry for her. He touched the knob with one finger, although his skill alone held it firm.

"Aye, there is." Through the darkened glass, the door of the connecting interrogation room suddenly swung wide and she strode in with a smirk on her face. "Forgot that door, didn't you?"

Damn it. He should have held that one in place too.

Sparks flared from her beautiful golden shifter eyes as she rounded the table and two metal-backed chairs. In dark jeans and a black cotton tank top that molded her breasts and slim waist, she halted before him and flicked the two-way intercom on. "Is there a reason you're hiding out from me again?"

"I'm not hiding from you."

"Then why bar me from entry, as well as to cease"—she plucked her cell phone from her pocket and waved it—"answering my calls?"

"There's a full moon tonight."

"I'm well aware there's a full moon, but I've still got one more month left until my bear comes into full maturity. That means you're safe from me tonight."

"I disagree."

"You are so frustrating." She arched one challenging brow. "You need a partner for your coming mission, and Murdock told me that partner is going to be me. We have a job to do today, so get yourself ready for it."

"The chief hasn't mentioned any coming mission to me." He'd need to speak to the chief after this interrogation was done. "The room you're in is needed. Leave now."

"You can't dismiss me that easily." She stuffed her cell phone back in her pocket and paced back and forth in front of the reflective glass, her long blond hair brushing her gloriously tight backside in those denim-hugging jeans, which truly should be outlawed on her. The denim even hugged her all the way to her cute ankles, her bare toes poking out from underneath the hem.

"You like my ankles?" Surprised, she stopped and stared right at him, not that she should have been able to make out exactly where he stood beyond the glass, or have even caught that particular emotional thought, not when his fae-skilled barriers were—damn, his guards weren't tight enough. He fixed that fast, strapped his shields fully into place and made certain she'd catch no more.

"Don't. You're blocking me and I hate it when you do that, or at least that completely. I'm an empath. We thrive on others' emotions and thoughts." She pressed her palm gently to the reflective glass, and he couldn't help but do the same.

"Bella, you truly do need to leave. I require the interrogation room and the chief will be here shortly to join me."

"I heard you the first time, and when he arrives, he'll update you on our coming mission. I want to leave within the hour, so don't be late."

"There isn't a chance I'm teaming up with you today." He shoved both his hands behind his back and clasped them there. His bear certainly wasn't happy about the glass standing between them, not when his beast clawed at his middle and tried to fight to get to the surface. "You're like fresh meat," he growled rough and low. "My bear likes fresh meat."

"I get that, but we have work to do, both of us, so let's keep it professional right now. I can manage a couple of days away in your company. Surely you can manage that in mine too."

"Where's Hunter?" Her brother always remained close to her on the night of a full moon, ensuring none of the unmated men fought over her.

"The chief sent him across the country on another mission. He's due back tomorrow morning and since you're the only man either Murdock or my brother truly trusts in the *keeping-your-hands-to-yourself* department, then you're honestly stuck with me tonight."

She nibbled on her lower lip and all he wanted to do was

shatter the glass between them and let his bear have a go at her. Unfortunately, she was right about him being the only one currently able to keep his hands off her, no matter how much he struggled to. Aye, all the unmated males in their clan wanted the mated bond with her, but only one lucky man would be able to lay claim to her in another month's time. "And what is our upcoming mission all about?"

"Murdock will update you." She winked at him, and far too mischievously for his liking. "I'll meet you upstairs, my bossy bear, right after my appointment with Liam. I'm awaiting some test results and want to check and see if they're in." With a wave and a sensual sway of her hips, she walked out and closed the door of the interrogation room behind her.

What test results? He flung open the side door and yelled, "Bella, wait."

"Later." She waved from the end of the panel-lined hallway and dashed upstairs.

"Bella!" He wasn't waiting until later to discover what test results she awaited from their resident doctor. He sprinted along the blue and green runner then skidded into Murdock as he rounded the corner. "Excuse me, Chief."

Blocking his path, his commander remained firmly in place. "Jamie, it's not right that one of my senior officers appears ready to flay an innocent lass."

"Bella is hardly an innocent lass, and I've no wish to flay her, just discover what might be ailing her. She's gone to see Liam to get some tests results. Is she ill?"

"She passed her medical last week, so no. It must be something of a personal nature that doesn't pertain to her ability to be one of our specialized team members." The chief ushered him back into the side room and shut the door behind him. In a navy button-down shirt and tan pants, his chief perched on the corner table and narrowed his gaze. "A new case has come in from our government operative. There's been a disturbance at the MacDonald's B&B along the Old Forest Road which weaves through the mountains. Forty-five minutes to the north of us. Gordon and Greer, the owners, were marking out a new forest trail for their guests when two bears came out of nowhere and charged them. They scrambled up the closest tree, then managed to remain there until nightfall when the bears finally wandered off. Clearly this kind of threat can't remain so close to their bed and breakfast."

"Bears, as in shifters like us?" No actual wild bears roamed their countryside any longer, although the odd one had been known to get loose from the safari park and other such wildlife sanctuaries, although they were quickly corralled and returned to their parks.

"Aye, shifters. Certainly no other bears have been reported missing, which is why this case has been passed directly onto us. Gordon and Greer are expecting both you and Bella at midday."

"I have an interrogation to soon oversee." He motioned through the glass.

"I'll take over here for you and have the interrogation interview taped. You can catch it on your return." Rising, Murdock pulled three vials from his shirt pocket and handed them to him. "A sedative, for the rogue bears."

"And the third vial?" He gave the deep orange concoction a swirl then slid the vials into the pocket of his black cargo pants.

"For you, if needed. A full moon rises tonight and with Bella's bear so close to full maturity, she's emitting some healthy and strong come-and-get-me pheromones."

"She's emitting far more than that."

"You'll survive, and Hunter and I both agreed you're the only one able to be around her tonight."

"I appreciate yours and Hunter's trust in me, but honestly, Hunter should be here himself if he wishes to keep any unwanted claws at bay. She's the only female so close to full maturity, one in amongst thirty-seven unmated males."

"Which is why I'm asking you to take her away from here tonight. This will give the other men a break. They all need it." Murdock opened the door and gestured him out. "Go and catch those rogues causing havoc and ensure they're contained. That's an order."

"Will do, Chief." He never disobeyed a direct order, never would either. Gritting his teeth, he left the room and took the side stairs leading to the third floor of Matheson Castle, his booted feet echoing on the stone stairs. Along the passageway, heavily paneled doors led off each side and a touch of the mid-morning sunshine streamed in through the far window overlooking the forest beyond their keep. At the last door on the right, he halted. Bella's chamber. His own rooms sat directly across from hers.

Resting one hand on the polished wood of her door, he leaned in and attuned his shifter hearing. No noise filtered through, although her sweet lily fragrance wafted all about. Memories stirred as he dragged her luscious scent deep into his lungs. He'd never forget the day she'd become an adult and left her family's quarters downstairs to take her own rooms across from his. A couple of years ago that had been now, and having her so close had both eased his bear's frustration and increased it. The frustration of course came from the fact she'd barrel in at any hour of the night, plop down on the end of his bed, wake him up and ask him how his day had gone. She fed off her loved ones' emotions just as those empaths within their clan always did. She needed personal contact, and lots of it.

He clenched his fists at his sides, his skin itching with the need to shift. His bear wanted out, to pin her down and claim her, no matter she was still a month shy of her soul bond forming with one of their unmated males.

With a heavy sigh, he pushed away from her door and opened his own.

With so few females born to them, the odds weren't in his

favor that Bella would be his, which meant he needed to keep his claws to himself until the truth became apparent. No matter who she might be bound to, it was his duty to ensure her protection, even from himself if needed.

Inside his chamber, he opened his desk drawer and slid his gun free. Their work was dangerous no matter the skills they held, and everyone within their specialized teams carried sufficient protection. It also appeared he'd soon be up against a couple of rogues, and they could get damn dangerous to deal with if they went wild as these two had quite possibly done.

At least they'd had no bears going wild like that within their own clan, not when they watched over each other so closely, although over the centuries a number of offshoot branches had separated away from theirs and contact had been lost, which meant rogues unfortunately existed, and in a number far greater than any of them liked.

Swiftly, he strapped on his holster over his honey-colored t-shirt and after ensuring the safety was set, slid his weapon into place and shrugged on his favorite battered denim jacket. On one knee at the end of his four-poster bed, he tugged out a slim wooden case from under the bed holding his most prized pieces and flipped the lid. He removed a jewel-encrusted dagger, one that had been passed down through the generations within his direct line—Nessa, the seer of ancient times' line. He traced one finger over the sapphire embedded into the hilt, the fine silver surrounding the large stone always gleaming bright.

He turned the blade over and stroked the matching sapphire on the other side. In his teenage years, when his father had bestowed this weapon to him, he'd said Nessa had first gifted it to her beloved grandson, who'd unfortunately passed away too soon from a terrible head and neck wound during a battle against their enemy. His father had even named him Jamie after that grandson, an honor for certain, and one he'd always tried to live up to.

Rising to his feet, he leaned over and lifted one cargo pant leg up and strapped the blade to his ankle. With another couple of weapons hidden on his body in his most favored places, he nabbed his duffel bag and tossed in some spare clothes in case this mission took longer than expected. He was always prepared for any eventuality, as all their highly skilled clansmen were.

Done and ready to leave, he opened his door and halted at the sight of Bella resting back against her own door, her tan leather jacket donned and her satchel propped on the floor. She'd pulled on footwear and now wore knee-high leather boots which hid those cute ankles of hers. "Did you do that on purpose?" He motioned to her boots.

"Aye, I couldn't have you getting all distracted during our mission with my cute ankles on display." She giggled, the tinkle of her laughter settling in his chest and warming it through.

"Tell me about the test results."

"What test results?" She winked. The damn tease. Whichever man would soon be mated to her was in for a hell of a ride.

Stepping up to the one woman his gut twisted for, he bit out, "Don't push me, Annabella Matheson. Are you ill?"

"I wouldn't be joining you on this coming mission if I was." She curled one hand into the cotton of his t-shirt and tugged him even closer. "And in case you've forgotten, don't call me Annabella in that angry way either. It hurts me when you do."

"I'm sorry." Empaths. They could be difficult to navigate around at times, so susceptible to any and every emotion, their own and everyone else's too.

"You've been avoiding me these past two weeks and keeping your distance. It hurts."

"You know I'd never intentionally set out to hurt you." He could kick himself for making her feel such pain. That had never been his intention. Only ensuring her safety from him had.

"Then cease keeping your distance and that hurt will stop."

"I'll try, but all the unmated males are on edge at the moment. You've got to give me a bit of a break." He snagged her satchel and slung it over his shoulder with his own. "We've got two rogue bears to corral, and not a lot of spare time to be chatting about these other issues. Let's go."

* * * *

Bella marched after Jamie, his second snub of the day hurting painfully. "Apart from the obvious reason, why else are you so angry at me? You smell just like Liam."

He released a low growl, but kept stomping on.

No one messed with Jamie when his bear got all snarly and ropeable as he currently was, only the empath in her couldn't stand his current foul mood, wanted only to soothe and calm him. Likely she was going about that in the wrong way, but today she just couldn't help herself. Something within her wanted to provoke him, to push him into this confrontation they both needed in order to get their issues resolved. She picked up her pace, darted past him then turned around at the top of the stairs and blocked his path. "Talk to me."

"Why is Liam angry at you? Did you go and wave your raging come-and-get-me pheromones around him as well?" He halted in front of her, leaned menacingly in and baring his teeth, snapped them together. "I can smell him all over you, which means you let him get too close."

"Are you jealous or something?" Their clan doctor was one of their unmated males and kept an office right here in the keep, his door always open for his kinsmen, although like all the other unmated males of late, he'd gotten territorial about her too, which meant aye, he'd gotten too close. All the single men wanted her covered in their scent and most pulled her into bone-crushingly tight hugs at every possible opportunity. Taking a shower was the only way to remove their scent, and she hadn't taken one since leaving Liam.

"What tests did you have done? Tell me, then I might not get quite so territorial."

"I'd rather not say and since they're in no way related to my ability to work on the mission field, I'm going to keep them to myself." Talk about an obstinate man. When he wanted to know something about her, he usually didn't cease harassing her until he'd uncovered that knowledge. It had always been that way with him. Even her brother, Hunter, would back off when she stuck to her guns, but never Jamie. "You've locked your chamber door each night these past two weeks and not allowed me in, so if I don't wish to let you in, you can't argue against that."

"If I'd allowed you into my chamber these past two weeks, then I wouldn't have let you back out again." He pushed forward with his body, corralled her right into the corner. With his hands planted either side of her head, he caged her in. "Does that scare you?"

"You'd never force me to do anything against my will, would cut off both your hands before you ever did that." She lifted her knee, went to stab her boot down on his foot, but he moved quick and breathing hard, pinned her knee to the wall.

"I might cut off my hands, but my bear wouldn't. He's so damn tired of remaining unmated, just as I honestly am." He lowered his voice to a deeply rough hue, a husky tone that made her inner bear claw to get closer to him. "Tell me what's wrong? If you're sick, I need to know."

"I'm not sick, but Liam needs to run more blood tests since he doesn't know quite what's wrong with me." Since it would help to calm him down, she might as well just tell him the truth even though it was a sensitive subject for her. "It's been four months since I had my last flow."

"And what will those blood tests show?"

"Liam needs to know if there's an imbalance in my hormone levels. He's wondering if my testosterone levels are too high, which means my body is getting mixed signals. Thus the lack of a flow."

"And what might cure those mixed signals?"

"In a normal human woman, one without fae-shifter blood, setting those levels back into line with the appropriate meds. With me, he's unsure. I've always been rather intolerant of regular meds."

"As we all are."

"We're different."

"Agreed, but in a good way." He nuzzled her neck, his voice dropping to an even huskier purr. "You smell ripe to me, Bella, as if you're ready to conceive. If you haven't had your flow, then it can't be far away. I'd all but guarantee it."

"That's what Liam said, that I smelt ripe for the taking too. He certainly can't scent my non-ovulating issues."

"Tell me exactly how close he got to you to scent that." He stroked one finger under her chin, tipped her gaze more fully to his and arched a brow. "Do you sense a bond forming with him?"

"I won't know who I'm soul bound to until the next full month." She pressed one hand flat against his rock hard chest and pushed him back. Thankfully, he relented and eased back a step.

"Just checking." He motioned for her to proceed him downstairs. "Let's move out. We honestly should get going. Two rogues to capture and all that."

Aye, they needed to get away, and she was kind of glad he appeared ready to drop this conversation. As he waited for her to go first, she walked past him and trotted downstairs.

Into the great hall, she strode then wandered around the perimeter toward the front door. Across the far side of the large vaulted room, the welcoming heat from the fire breezed through. Several of her clansmen sat lounging before the fire on a group of four comfy blue suede couches, Liam amongst them. He'd tossed his white lab coat onto the armrest and in his kilt and white shirt, waved out with the cheekiest grin.

Jamie growled yet again and snagged her hand, pulled her through the front foyer and outside onto the top step. On the other side of the inner bailey, a good thirty men wearing jeans or belted plaids had broken into pairs and with sweat gleaming on their bare chests, battled each other with their swords and shields glinting. All within their clan still adhered to the old ways even though modern technology had changed the world, and with their fae-shifter blood running so strong, the only way to expend their immense energy was with such intense training.

She surveyed the men, almost all unmated. One more month and she'd know which one of them would be her chosen one. She longed for that night, yet not the deep disappointment which would surely arise for those of her clansmen she didn't form a bond with. Life wasn't fair, not when their shifter clan now stood on the brink of extinction. More births were needed, particularly of the female variety so they could repopulate their clan.

Lifting her gaze to Jamie's, she kept her voice low and whispered, "I both long for the next full moon and fear it."

"So do I." He caught her elbow and steered her around the side of the keep along the cobbled path. "My bear needs a mate to settle down with."

She slipped through the postern gate where a guardsman stood at attention on the ramparts high above. Even though they had surveillance cameras positioned along the curtain wall at regular spaced intervals, they still kept physical eyes on their forested land and the long length of Loch Alsh running alongside it.

"Want to drive?" Jamie marched toward the closest black SUV parked in the rear lot, one of amongst a dozen or more gleaming SUVs. Dangling the keys in one hand, he opened the driver's door. "You always say I never give you the chance to drive when we head out."

"Thanks for the offer, but I'd rather you drive today. I'm feeling a little distracted and uneasy still from my conversation with Liam. I don't want to be a non-ovulating woman." She walked around to the passenger door, although he whipped around the hood and beat her to it. With a flourish, he opened the door. Hands on her hips, she glared. "Oh, so now you'll open a door for me?"

"You are in one feisty mood today." He tipped his head toward the seat. "Inside with you now and stop giving me so much sass."

"Sass is good for the soul." Smiling, she hopped in and strapped her seatbelt into place.

"So is a little Bella." Smiling back at her, he tossed their bags into the rear then slid behind the wheel, reached across the gears and squeezed her hand resting on her leg. "You truly do smell ripe to me. Like a luscious plum ready to be plucked from a tree, or maybe a strawberry dunked in chocolate and my teeth a mere breath away from sinking into it." He moaned and licked his lips. "Or even an ice cream waiting to be consumed on a hot summer—"

"Okay, okay, I get it." His heated words sizzled through her and as she looked into his eyes, she wanted only to drown in those shimmery golden depths. A few years ago, on the day she'd first reached adulthood, he'd been the one and only man to ever make her feel this hot and needy with just a few words alone. Aye, for years all she'd ever desired was to be closer to him. "Thank you for that rather descriptive analogy. It means a lot to me that you'd say all of that."

"You're welcome." He flicked the ignition on, tuned the radio to her favorite channel then turned the music down so it wouldn't blare too loud in their sensitive shifter ears.

"Not having a cycle is upsetting me. It makes me feel so out of sorts, like those times when our bears go into hibernation.

They're still there, but sluggish to awaken and bring forth."

"When was the last time you shifted? Perhaps that's part of the problem." Hands firm on the wheel, he drove along the winding gravel road lined with lush grass and wildflowers, the leafy elm trees growing either side of the road arching inward and creating a tunnel with a touch of sunshine dappling through the leaves overhead. The forest spread out for miles either side of their keep nestled right alongside Loch Alsh, the vivid tranquility of both the trees and the blue-green waters of the waterway so soothing. This was the most beautiful place on Earth, the only land she ever wanted to call home.

"It's been a month. I try not to shift too often, not when the men have been getting all riled up of late when I do. It isn't easy when my bear is hungering for her release to keep her contained." She lowered her window and rested her arm along the soft leather interior of the armrest. She tapped away. "I'd like to shift while we're away. It'll be easier on them and me if I do."

"Of course, and tell me what happened the last time you shifted, and be exact."

"Three of the men scented me and tore through the trees all snapping and snarling at each other. Mason even took a patch off Eli's butt."

"Ahh, so that's how that happened." He grinned, finding the humor in the situation, something she didn't mind at all. His small flare of joy helped to soothe her frazzled nerves further. "Eli has already healed, in case you're worried."

"I wasn't." Shifters healed far faster than mere humans ever could. "Will you shift with me? I need a playmate when I do, and Hunter and the chief trust you around me for a reason."

"At the moment, I don't trust myself so no, but I'll make certain your little bear has a chance to come out and play while we're away."

"Are you scared of me?" She tapped his nose then gasped as he caught her hand and nipped her fingertips.

"At present, I'm petrified of you." He released her hand just as quickly as he'd grabbed it.

"Yet I'm only half your size, so you shouldn't be."

"Half my size, but twice as dangerous."

"You love danger."

"Not when that danger comes in the form of a nearly mature female bear looking all peachy-perfect and ready for me to take a bite out of her." He caught her hand again, lifted it to his head and pushed her fingers into his shaggy dark locks. "I need a scratch."

"You would have had one well before now if you'd stopped locking your chamber door on me." Aye, shifters needed touch on a level unlike any other, particularly when it soothed their bears and lately she'd missed touching him since he'd pulled away from her.

As they left the sanctuary of Matheson land behind and joined the rumbling traffic on the main highway toward the village, she scraped her nails back and forth across his scalp. His dark hair was that exquisite shade of brown that held both a few strands of black and yet also gold, the three stunning colors matching his bear's pelt to perfection. In bear form, dark brown graced his back and sides, while golden hair covered his belly, and black tipped his ears and paws.

After each gentle scrape, she gave his locks a tug and his pleasure at her attention floated free and wrapped around her, just as the warm and spicy aroma of his delicious scent did. It made her bear roll around in the sweet elixir of it.

"Again," he growled, the low rumble making her belly flutter.

She slid her fingers deeper into his hair, curled her palm right over the top of his head then yanked on his hair far more forcefully.

"Mmm, perfect. Add the nails in too." His burning need emanated strongly from him, a need she couldn't ignore.

"Sometimes," she murmured as she scraped her nails deeper over his scalp then down his neck and under the collar of his denim jacket, "I struggle to understand why Isla first ran from her mate."

"She isn't running from Iain anymore." He drove past a gas station, where a white van and a red four-door passenger car filled up. Two children dashed across the forecourt, buzzed into the shop and eyed the candy section near the cash register.

"No, and now she's also pregnant and expecting two boys." Isla was one of her dearest friends and their chief's one and only child. They drove on, past rolling fields of lush grass. Up ahead, the stone steeple of a church rose high, the village's buildings on the main street lined up either side of it. "Murdock said Isla and Iain will be back tomorrow from Ivanson Castle. I can't wait to see her. She's been gone too long."

"I heard there's to be a feast held in celebration of her return." Jamie slowed as he drove through the quiet streets of the village and once they'd passed through the small settlement of stone and wattle-and-daub houses, he picked up his speed. "Do you want to go together?"

"That sounded suspiciously like you're asking me out, like on a date." Which he'd never done before, and never would unless they were in fact soul bound.

"You were complaining a few hours ago about how I've been evading you lately. I'm simply trying to make up for it." He followed the thinning, winding road up into the mountains.

"I don't do pity dates." The fresh air breezed through her open window and lifted her hair, tickled the strands across her skin and set her senses alight.

"You're getting all feisty again. You want to talk some more about your ovulation issues? Do you want me to be there when Liam takes your bloodwork?"

"Not if you're going to get all moody and aggressive on me as you did earlier in the hallway."

"You haven't even seen me get truly moody and aggressive yet." He caught her hand and settled it on his upper thigh, muttered, "I need more. Dig your nails in right here."

"Oh, I believe I have." She dug her nails deep into the muscled length of his upper thigh through the soft cotton of his black cargo pants.

He growled low again, with a far deadlier rumble.

Frowning, she raked her nails harder into his flesh. "Are you all right?"

"I might not be an empath, but I can sense your pain and worry about the men you won't form a bond with. My bear wants out, to stand in front of you and keep a strong guard, to take all your burdens onto his shoulders and to make certain you never have to fight whatever is about to come alone."

"He's one stroppy bear." She couldn't help but smile.

"He is around you."

"Let's talk about our coming mission instead of our joint stroppiness." A far safer topic, although even as she spoke the words, she stroked around to his inner thigh and dug her nails in there too. *Mine,* her stroppy bear grumbled within her. *Settle down,* she snapped back. *He's not ours unless the next full moon decrees that is so, and let's damn well hope it does since we both want him to be the one.*

"Sure, let's do that. Ladies first."

"Rumor about the keep is that your fae skill is strengthening." He held the ability of telekinesis, could move an object or even a person with naught but a mere thought from his mind alone. "Tell me everything, so I'm not surprised if I see those strengthening skills in action at the B&B."

"Nope, I'm not telling you a thing. I might need that element of surprise." He lowered his speed, the corners tightening as the road curved in and around the rising mountain path.

"Even against me?"

"Particularly against you." He indicated, turned off the Old Forest Road and entered a gravelly side road. They bumped over rutted tracks, the SUV managing the rougher terrain with ease.

Not a car in sight.

It was just them and the towering pines for as far as the eye could see.

"I'm hungry." He tipped his head toward the backseat. "Do you mind grabbing the emergency basket of snack food in the back? I missed breakfast."

"Not at all. One sec." She unbuckled her belt, bent back and heaved the wicker basket forward then buckled up again with the basket on the floor between her feet. She flipped open the lid and smiled at the offerings within. All prepackaged snack food, from beef jerky to protein bars and cheesy crackers. Bottles of water were propped to one side along with an assortment of her favorite Swiss chocolate bars. She extended one claw, sliced open the beef jerky and handed a long strip to Jamie before ripping open the wrapping of the chocolate bar and stuffing two pieces in her mouth. The creamy milk chocolate melted on her tongue and sent her taste buds into a frenzy. "Oooh, this is so delicious."

"Chocolate alone won't provide you with all the energy you'll need for this coming day. Have a protein bar."

"Wanna bet?" She popped another two pieces into her mouth as they bumped over the gravelly track leading ever deeper into the forest. The sweet explosion of decadence made her bear release a long purr deep inside of her. "My other half likes chocolate as much as I do. I also ate not long before we left. Eggs on toast."

"Good. You did better than me." He snagged a bottle of water and chugged half of it down.

"Are you a thirsty bear?"

"Aye, and more jerky please."

She tore off a bite-sized piece of jerky and grinning, waved it in front of his nose. "Is this what you want?"

"Pass it here, or I'll"—he jerked forward and snapped his teeth together, missing the jerky by an inch—"bite you too when I get it."

"You wouldn't dare." She waved the piece some more and he lunged and closed his mouth over the jerky and her two fingers.

Giggling, she tried to pull out of his grip except he sucked, his tongue rolling around both her and the jerky. With another bout of giggles, she popped her fingers free.

He eased back into his seat and moaned his pleasure as he chewed. "Now that's what I call delicious. Some Bella mixed in with my meat."

"You're such a naughty bear." She set a protein bar on his lap, which he unwrapped as he drove and ate.

Around the next corner, a quaint stone cottage emerged with smoke puffing from its chimney and horses whickering from within a high wooden beamed corral to the side. The forest rose sure and strong behind it, large pines that swayed in the brisk breeze. This place had always made a sweet playground for her bear.

"We're here." He pulled into the gravel parking lot in front of the MacDonald's B&B with its rustic front sign slightly titled just under the eaves over the front door. Ivy crept up one side of the main facade, while a cottage garden showcased a wide variety of flowering bushes planted along the other.

"The last time I came up here was when Hunter and I stayed with Gordon and Greer last summer." She'd always adored visiting this remote part of the Highlands, and Gordon and Greer were wonderful hosts, although thankfully quite unaware of their fae-shifter abilities. Very few outside of their clan knew of their true heritage, and that's the way things needed to stay.

Greer stood over a rose bush with pruning secateurs in

hand, her frilly yellow and white apron tied around her ample waist and a tightly furled red rose in hand. She walked over to Gordon, a stout man with gray hair who hammered in a marker into the soft soil at the end of the garden path. Greer set the rose on top and smiled softly, a wave of grief rolling from her, one that usually signified the recent loss of a beloved pet.

She pressed the window button and it whirred up.

"What's happening?" Jamie eyed her as he turned the key off.

"Let's give them a few minutes." She squeezed his arm. "They've lost a pet I'd say."

"Wait here then. I'll get your door and we can take in the air and see if we can pick up any traces of these bears we're after." He tucked his water bottle back in the basket, opened his door and jogged around to her side.

She accepted his offered hand, eased out and eyes closed, breathed deep as the fresh aroma of the forest swirled all around her. The crisp scent of the pines and the earthy notes of the land teased her senses, although Jamie's warm and spicy aroma overrode it all, his bear's fur-rich scent clinging to her since he stood so close. Oh aye, she could happily drown in his yummy fragrance. Eyes open, she smiled at him. "I can't scent any other bears, other than you."

"I can scent only your bear as well." He leaned over her, sank his nose into her hair and dragged in a deep breath. His bear rumbled deep within him, his chest vibrating as she pressed a hand against his heart. "You always smell so good, my sweet little bear."

"Well, you stink." She laughed and pushed against his chest. "Stop hovering."

"You're a terrible liar." He backed up a step, lifted his aviator sunglasses from the deep V of his honey-yellow t-shirt and slid them on. Surveying the area, he said, "With this place being so remote, the possible number of visitors to this area will thankfully be small."

"To bears though, the untamed forest surrounding this place would definitely call to their hearts." It certainly called to hers and Hunter's hearts whenever they'd visited.

"The Chief gave me three vials of sedative, said we were dealing with two rogues, but that I can use the last one on myself if I wish." Hands fisted at his sides, his claws suddenly sliced out and in, then out again.

"Hey, you don't need to do that." She caught one of his hands, traced over one extended claw.

"My bear is currently fighting the early stages of the coming full moon, which means by midnight when the moon hits it peak, I will need to sedate him. If I don't, you'll be his number one fascination, a meal tastier than any jerky or protein bar could ever be."

"Then we'll catch these rogues by then." Many of the unmated males struggled, but none ever stayed too close to let her see that struggle. They'd take off, let their bears go hunt for the night of the full moon and when they returned in the morning, they were back to being their usual selves.

"I also don't care to have you in the near vicinity of any rogues." He opened the rear door and snagged their bags from the backseat. With their satchels slung over his shoulder, he gestured for her to go first. "While we're here, stay close to me. Let's go."

She didn't move a step, just leaned back against the side of the SUV. "Hunter and the chief allowed us to team up for the night because they knew you could handle any distraction due to me. You should have more faith in yourself, just as they do."

"Your scent is far more than any simple distraction. It's an elixir of the most decadent sort."

"Yet I know you can handle it."

"No, Bella. I can't anymore." He swished his hands and she breezed off the ground. She lifted a full foot then grasped

Jamie's forearms as he stepped firmly in front of her and gave her one of his drilling stares.

"Hey, put me down before Gordon and Greer see me." She jabbed a finger downward. "This second, Jamie Matheson. Right now."

"Gordon and Greer have moved off into the stables and no one can see you with this vehicle in the way. I'll also put you down when I feel like putting you down." He slid one arm around her waist and tipped her back against the warm black metal before muttering, "This is a dangerous mission, with not only two rogues on the loose but me as well, and I'm one damn hungry unmated male after a bond. Don't take my warning lightly, Annabella."

"Bella. And I'm well aware you're one damn hungry male." She ran her hands up over his large biceps and curled her fingers around them. "Clearly you need to stake your claim while we're here. I understand why with two possible rogues so near, so whatever you need to do to calm your bear, then do it. Stake whatever claim you wish. Cover me in your scent, and if that's not enough, I give you permission to kiss me."

"I want to do more than saturate you in my scent." He nuzzled her neck, scraped his teeth back and forth across her pounding pulse point and sent all her thoughts scattering as he did. "I'm ravenous, have been walking an incredibly tight line around you of late."

"And I trust you to keep walking along that tight line and not to deviate from it." Certainly no man had ever made her feel so safe and secure as Jamie did, no matter the current frustration rising within him and leaking past his guards. "I wouldn't mind if you took me up on my offer though. Smother me in your scent and kiss me."

She'd been dreaming of how he'd kiss her, how he'd touch his lips to hers and share the same breath as her.

His gaze narrowed and that delicious rumble vibrated again

in his chest and rose upward. It left his throat in a snarly rasp and she couldn't help but tighten her grip on his arms. Still floating, she leaned in and rubbed her body against his. "I dare you to kiss me."

"Careful, Bella. You're treading into dangerous territory."

"And you're not treading into it quite fast enough." She wanted more from him, and she'd wanted more for a while. "Do it," she whispered. "Kiss me, Jamie Matheson."

Chapter 2

The year 1211, a week before Jamie's death and Annabella's ascension with Cherub beyond the veil.

"Do it," Annabella whispered. "Kiss me, Jamie Matheson."

Annabella stared Jamie down as he stood in his battle leathers at the sea-gate landing. Certainly no man had ever made her itch for more the way Jamie did, no matter the frustration that also arose within her whenever he was close. "We're mated, due to wed in another fortnight and still you willnae kiss me."

"You should never dare one who holds the 'power of thought,' Annabella." Jamie turned his back on her, released his skiff's mooring rope, coiled and tossed it into the center of the hull then slid another aggravated look at her over his shoulder.

"Dinnae call me Annabella in that angry way. I've warned you afore no' to do so." She remained stoically in place, her hands on her hips and her gown's red woolen skirts beating against her legs in the brisk sea breeze. "Jamie, we're mated, betrothed and soon to be wed, but you seem so intent on no' spending any further time with me between now and our wedding day. I'm an empath. I can sense your emotions and your frustration smothers me."

"Kissing is for wedded couples, Annabella. We have another fourteen days until we speak vows. I willnae bring any dishonor down upon your head by taking more from you than I currently should." He jabbed a finger at the keep rising high behind her. "Back inside with you now."

"I won the wager between us last eve, and you promised me that if I did you'd take me to the caves farther along the loch. I long to see the place which your parents so often speak about, and the only way there is if I tread across the boggy marshland, which I've no intention of doing, no' when you're already sailing alongside the coastline in that direction. Please, take me."

"Your brother willnae permit any man to be alone with you, and night will soon fall. 'Tis only a mere few hours away."

"Do you see my brother here right now?" She waved a hand around the landing devoid of even one soul. Not even the guardsmen patrolling the battlements could be seen, although they'd be there, somewhere. "My brother's ridden out for the headland to take over the point watchman's duty and willnae return until the morrow. Now is the only time I can go. Please." She laid a hand on his arm, his large bicep going taut and hard under her fingers. "Will you no' keep your word?"

"I always keep my word." Gritting his teeth, he gestured to his skiff. "In with you then, afore I change my mind."

"Thank you." With a grin of success, she swished past him, clambered on board and eased onto the bench seat at the stern.

"You may have won this argument, but you willnae win the next." Grumping under his breath, he nabbed the oars, sat on the center seat and stuck them into the swell and rowed. Once he'd passed the breakers, he tucked the oars away, seized the ropes and raised the sail. The wind filled it with a vigorous slap and with his booted feet braced wide along the side of the skiff, he steered his boat alongside their Matheson land as he negotiated the rough waters toward the headland.

She rested her arms on the edge of the skiff and took in the rugged coastline where the forest butted right up to it. Sparrows twittered from high in the treetops while seagulls pranced along the foreshore, beaks stabbing the muddy flats in search of a tasty treat. The hills rose high into the distance and a waterfall graced the dip in one prevalent peak. With a soft sigh, she smiled. "This is the most beautiful place in the Highlands."

"I wholeheartedly agree."

"Thank you for bringing me with you."

"I hardly had a choice." A gruff answer, one she couldn't help but grin at.

As they sailed, he tightened his hold on the ropes, his black leather pants sitting low on his hips, the soft leather molding his muscled thighs and backside, his claymore sheathed on one hip and his dagger on the other. Two large sapphire stones were embedded in the dagger's fine silver hilt and engraved with his name.

"You seem to be mightily fascinated by my weapons, wee Annabella."

Heat flushed her cheeks and she pressed her hands to them. "I was actually admiring both you and your weapons." She pushed to her feet and swayed as they crested a wave and splashed down.

"Come here." Jamie swept one hand out, nabbed her around the waist and pulled her up hard against his chest. "Hold onto me. The waters roughen and I hardly need you falling overboard."

She wrapped her arms around his middle and with his feet once again planted wide along the side of the skiff, he tugged on the ropes and steered them alongside the coastline through the white-tipped swell. "Nessa told me once, that you were in fact born on the water. Is that true?"

"Aye, my grandmother only ever speaks the truth."

"Tell me how that came to be, you being born on the water and all."

"Nessa had a vision the morn of my birth and immediately set out to warn my parents, only she missed their leaving by a mere few minutes. Father had decided to take Mother aboard his skiff to the very caves where we're headed toward now." He glanced at the shoreline. "Her waters broke as they sailed into the bay up ahead."

"And he didnae decide to turn around and sail his skiff back to the keep?" She tucked a lock of his dark wind-tossed hair behind his ear, her fingers tingling where she touched his skin.

"There wasnae time." Holding the sail's rope with one hand, he spread his other hand more firmly over her lower back.

"Tell me more." Her breath came faster, his as well. "Your mother clearly delivered you safely."

"Aye, and at my father's hand no less. While in the bay, the waters so calm that day, he lowered the sail and intended on rowing them in, only my mother cried out and he instead laid his furs in the hull for her to rest upon. Apparently I was beyond eager to enter this world and she gave birth to me within mere minutes." His hand dipped lower, right over her bottom.

"Then what happened?" She raised her arms, twined them around his neck, her fingertips playing in the longer length of his hair brushing his shoulders. Never had she touched him so intimately, but this moment was theirs alone and she had no intention of losing it.

"They named me James in honor of my uncle who'd passed away in battle the year afore." He groaned and squeezed her bottom. "You feel so good against me."

"You feel good against me too." She couldn't miss the bulge in his pants and the heavy presence of it pressing into her belly. Even though she was an innocent, she wasn't exactly unaware of what happened between a man and woman, not when she'd stumbled across her fair share of warriors coupling with wenches in all manner of places about the keep. From darkened nooks within passageways, to the storeroom and the stables.

Once she'd even been walking in the forest late one night and caught sight of an amorous couple together in the woods. Likely she shouldn't have remained, but instead she'd ducked behind a thick tree trunk and held her breath as the pair stood kissing under the gentle glow of the moon at the edge of a small clearing. The man had soon left the lass's lips though, trailed his mouth down her neck and along the upper swells of her breasts. He'd popped her full mounds free of her bodice, sucked ravenously on her nipples before toppling her to the lush grass underfoot and diving under her kirtle's brown skirts. The lass's eyes had near rolled to the back of her head as pleasure had consumed her then moments later, the man had lifted free of her, thrust his cock inside her and the two had come so fast in a loud and boisterous cry.

Aye, that was the kind of love she wanted with Jamie, a love which couldn't be halted no matter where they might be. She pushed her fingers deeper into his hair and rubbed his scalp.

"What are you doing, Annabella?" His low growl vibrated with neediness.

"I would hope that would be obvious." Smiling, she reached up on her toes, her lips a mere breath from his. "Please kiss me, Jamie. I want to know what it feels like to share the same breath as you. Dinnae deny me any longer."

Chapter 3

"I won't fall for any dare, particularly not issued from your sweet lips." Jamie shook his head as he tried to clear it, only Bella had gripped his arms and wasn't letting go, or maybe that was him who wasn't letting go of her, where he'd pressed her up hard against his SUV.

"We've never kissed, and I—" She rubbed her hips against his hips, her golden shifter eyes burning bright. "Please, Jamie. I want to know what it feels like to share the same breath as you."

"You're letting your feisty female bear rise too close to the surface. You only want to kiss me because there's a full moon on its way, and no matter you've a month left until you're ready for a bond to form, your bear is still clamoring for some attention." He pressed her even harder against the black metal, her golden locks cascading over her shoulders like a river of satin. "Likely a kiss from any of the unmated males within our clan right now would work for you."

"No, I want a kiss from you, and only you." She released his arms, snagged the collar of his denim jacket and held on tight. "I promise not to tell Hunter, or anyone else about this."

"Any one of the thirty-seven unmated men in our clan could be your chosen one, and I'm not permitted to kiss you when you might very well belong to another."

"Yet you're the only one I want to kiss and right now, your emotions are ramming into me so hard I can barely think straight. You want to touch me, to bite me. I can sense your desire and it's sending my bear into a spin. She wants you, just as I want you."

"So she likes it when I get all aggressive and unwilling?" He pushed the sides of her tan leather jacket out of the way, gripped the hem of her black tank top and lifted it high enough to expose her belly. Gently, he stroked the creamy soft skin of her midriff and hopefully embedded enough of his scent into her flesh to calm his inner beast down.

"We both like it when you stake your claim, just as you're doing now. Making sure I hold your scent is reassuring, but if you kissed me or bit me, that claiming could go even deeper."

"You shouldn't be asking me for my bite." He dropped her top, touched the back of one of his hands to the soft curve of her cheek, trailed his fingers along her jaw then softly collared her throat. "No matter I like it that you did."

"Only like?"

"Damn it, more than like." He kicked her legs apart and pressed every hard inch of himself against her as he kept her levitated at his height. "Say my name."

"Jamie." She gripped the waistband of his pants, her thumbs sliding under his t-shirt's hem then gently, she stroked over his hips in small circles with her thumbs.

"That's it. Take in more of my scent." His bear clawed for release, to topple her to the ground and dominate her, only that he'd never be able to do.

"And here I thought you didn't want to play with a female bear on the cusp of entering into full maturity." She stroked higher, lifting the hem of his shirt as she glided up his sides and over his pecs. With a stuttered breath, she touched her midriff to his belly, her golden shifter eyes blazing with fire.

"More skin." He couldn't keep the demand from his voice. He trailed his fingers down her silky neck, dipped into the gap between her full breasts exposed by her black tank top then back up again. With his other hand, he roamed down her back and cupped her curvy backside.

"I think I'm well and truly covered in your scent now." She licked her lips, and he followed the sensual swipe of her tongue with his gaze. She had the lushest mouth, smart and sassy too.

Staking his claim and kissing her right now rode him hard. "Tell me to stop if I go too far."

"The word stop won't be leaving my lips in the next few minutes. That I can assure you."

* * * *

Wanting more, Bella wrapped her arms around Jamie's neck and drew his head closer to hers, until his mouth hovered a mere breath away. Such a raw and primal need roared through her, made her breasts swell and her nipples scrape against the cotton of her bra. She wanted her top and bra off, until every inch of his masculine skin slid warmly against hers. "Do you feel it, Jamie?"

"Aye, I can feel every inch of you." Another husky rumble of need made heat flare in her core and gather between her thighs.

She lugged in a breath.

She had no words for how sublime this moment was, so instead she leaned farther back against the vehicle, her neck angled so should he wish to take her up on her offer and bite her, then he'd know beyond a doubt that he'd had her permission first.

"Damn it, Bella. You're so incredibly enticing." He stroked one finger down her neck, right along the exposed skin she offered him.

"You have my consent."

"I'm well aware I do."

"You're also taking far too long in accepting my offer."

"I won't bite you, but I am going to—" He swooped in, covered her mouth with his and the shock of his lips finally on hers sent a spear of such intense pleasure coursing through her. Then he pulled back a touch and gentled his kiss, his lips brushing so tender and feather-light over hers.

"Bite me, in the way of those who are soul bound do," she whispered against his lips and almost drowned in the open desire swarming within his eyes. "On my neck. Now."

"That spot is reserved only for your mate, of which you've yet to discover who that truly is."

"Lift me higher." Hands fisted in his hair and his gloriously warm and spicy scent rolling all around her, she tried to get her way.

"Give me a moment." With his hands cupping her bottom, he lifted her with both his grip and his fae skill. "Have you ever allowed another to touch you like this?"

"That question is irrelevant." Although she hadn't, not when she'd only ever wanted him.

"Your scent is intoxicating, and making my bear drunk with the need for more."

"Then take more."

"You need to cease giving me whatever it is I want." He kissed her again, then just as quickly pulled back. "I should stop."

"One more kiss." She dipped her mouth to his neck, trailed her lips along his jaw and nipped and nibbled as she did.

"I can scent Gordon." He yanked back and dropped her fast.

"Pardon?" Dazed, she breathed deep and tried to slow her frantically beating heart.

"I said I can scent Gordon. He and Greer have left the stables, although Greer's taken the pathway to the back door while he's waiting at the front." He righted her tank top then fixed his own shirt, picked up their bags which he'd dropped and marched toward Gordon. "Strap on your tranquilizer," he muttered over his shoulder with one last glance at her.

"Sure." She opened the glove compartment in the SUV, pulled the weapon out and holstered it. As she did, she tried heartedly hard to tamp down her current frustration. Kissing her partner while on a mission truly wasn't acceptable, although it appeared neither she or her bear currently wanted to listen to reason.

Composing herself as best as she could, she followed Jamie across the graveled yard toward Gordon as he waited next to the door with its welcoming potted ferns planted either side of it in bright yellow pots.

The elderly man's lips lifted in a smile.

"Good to see you, Gordon." Jamie extended his hand and shook Gordon's. "I hear you and Greer ended up in a tree for some hours due to two bears."

"Aye, we were marking out a new walking track for our guests due to arrive this coming weekend." He motioned toward the trail entrance at the edge of the forest where a red ribbon fluttered on a length of wood staked into the ground. "None of our visitors though shall be able to use it, not until this immediate threat is removed. We called the authorities this morning, the moment we returned and were told a team from Matheson Castle would arrive soon. Glad to see it's you and Bella."

"We'll find those two bears and ensure they're captured and contained. Likely they've gotten loose from the safari park."

"Maybe even the wildlife zoo," she added helpfully as she joined them. She patted the tranquilizer gun she'd strapped to her side. "We're armed and dangerous, and we'll get them rounded up and out of here, Gordon."

"Good. Bears haven't been spotted within these woods for centuries, and we don't need these ones getting any closer to home than they already have, not with the horses we keep corralled here. They'll remain in the stables until you've eliminated the threat."

"Of course, and we'll find them." Of that she had no doubt, not when Jamie was one of the best trackers in their clan, right alongside Hunter.

"I understand you'll be staying the night." Gordon opened the door and motioned them inside. "Greer's readying your rooms for you both right now."

"Wonderful." She stepped over the threshold in her boots then walked across the tan and cream striped carpet to the guest ledger open on the slim rosewood front table with its elegant silver-stemmed lamps sitting on either side. With the slim black pen in hand, she scrawled her name and Jamie's in the register then nabbed a mint from the glass bowl next to it and popped it in her mouth.

"Hello, my dears. I see you've signed in." Greer walked down the stairs from the landing above, her fluffy white slippers scuffing the carpet and her white cardigan draped over one arm. Like a fresh breeze, she blew in and smothered her in a motherly hug. "'Tis good to see you again, my dear Bella. How's your brother?"

"Hunter's well, although away at present, which is why I've come with Jamie instead."

"You're both welcome to come and stay whenever you please. I've already set the white room aside for you, your favorite since it looks out over the meadow and forest out back." To Jamie, she smiled warmly and said, "Your room is beside Bella's, the one you stayed in last time. Hunter prefers that room too. Dinner will be at seven sharp. Does that suit?"

"Thank you, that suits perfectly, will certainly give us the entire afternoon to scour the woods." Jamie set a hand at Bella's back. "We'll go settle in then leave for the hunt. We'd like to get outside as quick as we can." He guided her past the large urn of purple and pink flowering azaleas and up the stairs bordered by a white-painted wall on one side and a rosewood banister on the other.

Portraits of Gordon and Greer's adult daughters lined the stairwell and at the top, a large family portrait hung in a glorious silver frame, one showcasing their five grandchildren sitting around them on a bench in the forest. She slowed and touched the cool silver of the frame. "Have you ever met Gordon and Greer's daughters?"

"No, have you?"

"Of course. If you come and stay during the holidays, you'll meet them too." She continued on down the carpeted hallway, opened the door into the white room and held out her hand for her bag. "I can carry it from here."

"I'm sure you can." He stepped forward and she backed up into the room since she didn't care to get knocked over by him. With a narrowed gaze, he scanned her room as if ensuring all remained secure before he set her satchel on top of the queen-size bed covered in a white crocheted comforter with plush golden-trimmed white pillows at the headboard.

"Surely you're not expecting the rogues to be in here?" She crossed her arms and raised a brow. "Try and relax a little, Jamie."

"I might be on edge, but that's a good thing. It'll keep my senses on full alert." He ambled around to the tall window framing the head of the bed where the golden drapes had been secured with golden tassels then with one finger, eased the white net curtain aside and surveyed the stables and forest beyond.

"Does everything look clear?" She plopped down next to her bag on the bed, eased her tan leather jacket from her shoulders and unzipped her knee-high boots. With the top flap of her satchel unbuckled, she rummaged inside and removed a pair of ankle-high riding boots perfect for the outdoors and trekking along the damp forest trails. Boots laced, she unpacked the remainder of her belongings into the white-painted wooden drawers.

"All is clear."

"Give me a second then." She ducked inside the adjoining bathroom she'd be sharing with Jamie, his room on the opposite side of the connecting door. Hunter usually took that room, which brought a smile to her face. Her brother was about to miss out on an intriguing hunt to track down two rogues. He'd love to be here and a part of this current case.

Mmm, and this bathroom had the most decadent bathtub with jets and all. Usually she had to get in here quick at the end of the day to beat Hunter to it. Gently, she ran a finger along the curved edge of the white porcelain, fairly buzzing at the thought of the bath she'd enjoy tonight. An array of deliciously scented soaps and bubble baths sat within the holder at one end and she plucked the sweet lily scented bottle free, her favorite and one she always used at home. "I bags the bathroom first tonight," she called over her shoulder. "I'm dying for a long, hot soak."

"Sure." He stepped inside the luxurious bathroom, removed his toiletries from his bag and set them on the vanity's counter then opened the other door and disappeared inside his room.

She followed him, leaned against the doorway while he looped his bag over the high-backed chair in front of the corner oak writing desk. He strolled across to the large bed with its brown furs and padded leather headboard. The crisp scent of the woods wafted in through the open window above it, the teasing fragrance from outside making her inner bear stir to full wakefulness. "Are we going to talk about that kiss?"

"There isn't much to talk about. We kissed and that's it." He cocked one brow at her, his words so gruff.

"I've never wanted to kiss anyone, other than you." Surely that meant something. It did to her. She rubbed her neck, along the spot where she'd desired his bite too. "I've also never asked another for their bite."

"I'm honored you asked for mine, but as yet I've no right to give it." Pain laced his tone as he walked back to her, caught her face in his hands and looked deep into her eyes. "One more month, Bella, then we'll know for certain who you belong to, and of course…who belongs to you."

"I hope that man is you." Whispered words as she covered his hands with hers. "Thank you for the kiss earlier. I liked it, a lot." Although since they truly needed to be away, she backed up from him. "We have two rogue bears to track down and before seven no less. I don't want to miss out on one of Greer's meals."

"Neither do I." All brisk, he nodded and walked to the door leading to the hallway and opened it.

She strode past him and walked downstairs then hiked it out the front door into the midday sunshine, Jamie one step behind her. This man had haunted her dreams since the day she'd moved into the rooms across from his chamber, and over the past few years whenever she'd knocked on his door and blown on in, she'd never felt more at peace than when she'd been with him.

"Let's catch us a couple of big bad bears." With one hand at her back, he steered her along the cobblestone pathway around to the stables.

They passed the horses whinnying within the wooden-beamed corral and she re-attuned her acute shifter hearing so she'd pick up any and all sounds. Birds chirped and insects buzzed. The leaves of the trees rustled and somewhere close by, the splashing of the fast-flowing river which meandered right through these mountains traveled to her. She trekked past the red flag stabbed in the ground and strolled along the forested trail that Gordon and Greer had found the bears down. Breathing deep, she searched through the multitude of fragrances in the air for the one which would lead her directly toward their prey. Only she got nothing. "I'm not picking up any other bears, other than you."

"Same. Let me move on ahead of you so I can track a little better. Your scent is overwhelming my senses." With his black cargo pants cupping his tight backside, he jogged ahead and nose to the air, breathed deep as he foraged through the pine-fresh aroma swirling all about them.

Small critters scampered through the dense underbrush, likely dashing away at the clear presence of the predator now amongst them. Not unusual, not when Jamie—even in his human form—emitted the distinct scent of an immense bear. Aye, he was all alpha, all male, all bear, every wickedly muscled inch of him.

She breathed deep and drew in his heady aroma, his fur-rich scent mixed with a spicy undertone that made her nipples stiffen and her mouth dry out for more of a taste of him. Her breath came harder and she halted, bent half over and tried to clear her mind of the dizzy haze striking her. Oh boy, the coming full moon was certainly working a number on her.

As her cell phone beeped, she straightened and pulled it out of her jeans pocket. An incoming message from the chief. Jamie halted up ahead, then ducked into the scrub off to one side and scouted about.

She leaned back against the nearest trunk and opened the message.

Keep Jamie in sight.

She messaged the chief back. *Did you have a vision?*

His returning answer blared an instant later. *Aye.*

Want to elaborate? She hit send.

Can't, but stay on your toes.

"A message just came in from the chief," she called out as she pushed off the tree. "You got anything yet, Jamie?"

"I just caught a whiff of one of the rogues. What did the chief's message say?" He shuffled out of the scrub, jogged back to her and snuck her cell phone from her hand. He grimaced as he scanned the chief's words. "Murdock is being elusive again."

"Isn't he always?" Their chief always took great care when he received visions, particularly when as a seer, he detested altering their future to any great degree, or at least any more than was absolutely necessary. He believed in free will, that one needed to make their own choices in life, but when it came to his kin, he also believed in keeping them safe. Never would he allow any harm to befall them. Thus the message, even as elusive as it was. *Keep Jamie in sight.* She certainly would.

Eyes closed, she tightened her shields as Jamie's worry barreled into her, then thankfully he firmed his shields and the outpouring of his anxiety over her eased. As it did, she opened her mind once more to the forest beyond them and attempted to find even a trace of any emotion leaking from anyone else who might be in their near vicinity.

"Are you all right?" He tucked her cell phone back into her pocket and pulled her into a hug. Gently, he rubbed her back.

"I'm fine, just focusing. We have to make sure these rogues don't return and chase any other innocent visitors up trees. This wilderness is here for everyone to enjoy."

"Agreed." He firmed his hold on her, mushing her face right into his honey-yellow shirtfront.

"You're making me feel incredibly claustrophobic, Jamie. Can you let me go?"

"No, I can't. Give me a moment."

She waited out far more than a moment, not that she was truly complaining. High in the canopy overhead, the afternoon sunshine speckled through the vibrant green foliage of the pine trees, and along one branch a pretty Scottish crossbill with brown-tipped feathers pecked at a dangling pine cone.

"When the chief says *keep Jamie in sight*"—he rubbed his chin over the top of her head—"it's a double message. That means I need to keep you in my sight as well."

"Show me what drew your interest in that scrub over there." She gestured to the bushes. "I want to see if I can pick up one of the rogue's scent like you did."

"I'll show you where he's trampled about near the scrub."

He caught her hand and led her to the bushes, hunkered down before the largest bush and pressed one palm against the dirt at the base. Claws slicing out and in, he touched a padded footprint and looked back at her over his shoulder. "This mark is fairly fresh. It'll be best if I made the Change. That way I can better hunt these rogues."

"I'll hold your clothes while you shift."

"Thank you." He removed his boots and treasured dagger, his other weapons and jacket, then whipped his t-shirt over his head and dropped it into her hands.

The golden skin of his chest gleamed, the rippling strength of his muscled torso making her fingers itch to touch him. And oh, what a sinfully delicious trail of hair he had arrowing down his belly and disappearing within the waistband of his pants. She wanted to touch him there, so bad.

Belt unbuckled, he eyed her with one questioning brow raised. "Are you going to turn around?"

"If I have to." A croaky answer. Whenever any of her kinsmen shifted, they always looked away to give each other the most privacy they could, although even so she'd seen Jamie make the Change many a time, had witnessed his big bear bursting forth in a beautiful display of sparkling lights, although never this close and never had she allowed her gaze to wander below his waist when she had. With the full moon's looming pull though, when she tried to turn around, she couldn't. "I don't seem to be able to move. Do you mind shifting behind the tree?"

"She's getting bolder, isn't she?"

"Aye." She licked her lips as he strode around her and out of her sight behind the trunk.

"My bear's getting bolder too. You'll need to keep an eye on him, Bella. If he gets too pushy or forceful, take him to task."

Rustling resounded, and her pulse raced, the wind whisking around her and bringing with it Jamie's deliciously spicy scent. It overrode all else and eyes closed, she drew his intoxicating aroma even deeper into her lungs, until it filled her and sent her senses into a whirlwind.

"Stay very still." His voice whispered from right behind her, then slowly he ran one hand down the long length of her hair, gripped her hips and chin on her shoulder, rubbed his nose against her neck. "Tip your head more fully to the side."

"You're supposed to be making the Change."

"I'm ready to do so, stark-naked and all." A gruff growl. "Do as I said."

His commanding demand rolled through her in the most decadent way, and ever so slowly, she stretched her neck to one side, beyond eager for whatever he intended.

"You're making my need for you heighten to the worst level." He trailed one finger along her pulse point then pressed his lips there. "Keep your neck exposed once I've shifted. It'll appease my bear a little."

"Aye, sir."

"Don't *sir* me. You're such a tease." He shifted, so fast and she spun about as the crackling energy and sizzling display of light shimmered all around.

His big bear heaved up onto his hind legs and roared, his fur a dark chocolate brown, his paws and ears tipped with black and his belly rippling a golden shade. He thumped back down and prowled toward her, his teeth snapping together and claws digging into the pine-needle covered trail.

She backed up, knocked her back against the trunk behind her and flung her hands up. "Jamie, wait. Don't you dare hurt me or I'll be forced to have words with you."

He surged up again, slammed his paws down on the bark either side of her head, his belly exposed as he bellowed fiercely.

She clapped her hands over her ears as his growl thundered all around, his warning clear to hear. That he wouldn't permit any others near her and should any trespass on this place and moment in time, he'd slay them. "Jamie, quieten down. We're on a hunt and we want to find these rogues, not send them running from us."

Muzzle shoved into her neck, he sniffed then rubbed his furry cheek against her cheek.

She grasped the trunk harder, tried to hold herself upright only she lost her grip and slipped, barely managed to grab him around his furry neck before hitting the ground. Dangling underneath him, her hair swishing across the forest floor, he wedged his snout against her neck. She couldn't help but smile. "Oh goodness, stop pushing me around, my bossy bear."

Howling on all fours, he lowered his head further until he'd set her safely down on the ground on her back then with one beefy paw, his strength so immense, he rolled her over onto her belly and sniffed down her body, from her head to her toes. He missed not a spot.

"Are you checking me over?" Sexy bear. She rolled over and tried to get farther away, only he stomped after her, planted his paws in the way and stuck his muzzle into her belly.

A low whine, one asking if she was all right.

"I'm not hurt, but I am now dirty thanks to you." She pushed her hands into his silky pelt, right around his neck and gave him a little shake. "We have two bears to find."

Nose to the air, he snorted as if searching for those very bears, each of his legs bracketing her body as he took a terrifyingly protective position. With a deadly snarl, he bared his teeth.

"You've caught something more?" She sniffed the air too, and this time caught a whiff of a bear on the breeze and scrambling around underneath him, ducked her head out.

Another fierce roar and he charged off.

Two massive gray bears pounded through the underbrush toward them.

Keep Jamie in sight

She wouldn't let him fight this oncoming battle alone. She

shucked her clothes and made the Change, her bones and limbs burning at the excruciating speed of her shift, but with her bear released she could help even up the odds. She chased Jamie, her bear skidding in the mossy earth underfoot, while ahead, he heaved up and sailed through the air. He came down hard on both rogues at the same time, blood spurting and his claws as razor sharp and deadly as any sword he could wield.

Bellowing, he sank his teeth into the neck of the first bear then stamped on the other's body and bones snapped. He reared back, ready to hit both bears again but both lay motionless on the mushy ground. Never had she seen such strength emanating from him before.

She pounded across and butted her head into his flank.

He pushed her back with his big body, away from the downed rogues, his shifter-bright eyes glaring as he snapped out a grizzled command she understood well.

He wanted her away from them. Right now.

Not happening. She was his backup and would remain so, but since the rogues were down, she could leave him for a minute, and only long enough so she could nab her cell phone from her clothes and call this in to the chief.

She loped back to her scattered belongings, shifted and dressed and with her cell phone in hand, fired off a quick text message then jogged back to Jamie with his clothes. She set his belongings in front of him, swiftly pulled two of the three vials of sedative from his cargo pants pocket and muttered, "I sent a message to the chief. You shift and I'll administer the sedatives."

In a crackling blaze, he made the Change, and she barely whipped around in time as he did. "How'd you tackle them both so fast?" she said as she knelt next to the first rogue.

"I've gotten stronger in the use of my telekinesis, managed to thump both their heads together before I dropped down on top of them." Shuffling as he dressed.

"You can move multiple objects at once now?" Never had

she witnessed him doing so before, and certainly not anything quite the size of these beasts. "Clever bear."

"Thank you." He leaned over her, clothed again as he lifted the drooped head of the first rogue and she dripped the sedative in. The beast grunted, tried to snap his teeth as he became more aware, but Jamie swished his fingers and the animal whimpered, jaws going slack. "A little squeeze to the skull never hurt anyone."

"I never thought we'd find them this fast."

"Neither did I." He motioned for her to move to the other bear.

She shuffled across, lifted the head of the second rogue, swished the orange concoction and spilled the vial's contents into the animal's mouth then settled his head back on the ground.

"Good work." He scooped her up and set her back down on her feet farther away from the bears.

"They're down and can't hurt me." She handed him the empty vials which he pocketed.

"They were after you, must have been able to scent the come-and-get-me pheromones you're emitting. Your scent is strong, and only growing stronger."

"You're saying I'm a wanted woman?"

"You're so close to coming on heat. One more month and you'll be twice as difficult to be around."

"I like being difficult."

"I'm sorry they interrupted us just before." He caught her hand, lifted her arm and inspected it before lifting the other and gliding his fingers along her skin. "Not a scratch in sight. At least the other unmated males at home won't beat me up for not looking out for you quick enough."

"They came at us fast, with no warning at all." The fur-rich scent of his bear crashed into her, his rising emotions as well. It all caught her up in its intensity, his words of earlier that she keep her neck exposed to him making her tip her head to the side and expose her neck to him now. She gave him a wink. "I believe this is where we were."

"You don't need to do that now." Gaze narrowed, he stepped back from her. "My bear is once again leashed."

"Ugh, you are so aggravating sometimes." Her cell phone beeped and she plucked it from her pocket and checked the screen.

"What does it say?" He kept the bulk of his body between her and the downed rogues.

"Two government operatives are choppering in. ETA twenty minutes. Manning and Sutherland. The chief said good work, fast and speedy."

"I'm familiar with Manning and Sutherland. Are you?"

"I've met them a time or two." The iron-rich scent of blood permeated the air and overrode the freshness of the pines and the earthiness of the damp soil, made her wrinkle up her nose in distaste. "I don't like how they smell."

"Something's wrong with their blood." He gestured toward the trail. "You go and meet the operatives at the B&B and bring them in."

"I'll be as quick as I can."

"Wait." He caught her hand, dipped his head to her neck and snarling, licked her flesh, right over her pounding pulse.

"Jamie." She kept her tone a commanding one. "Do what you need to do. I understand the full moon's pull and your current frustration."

"I'm not allowed to bite you, but I do need to kiss you again. Is that permissible?" Rumbling deep in his throat, he captured her mouth before she could answer and kissed her deeply, his body a fiercely hot brand against her own as he took command of the moment.

She graciously gave in, nearly swooned into him.

Oh goodness. Jamie Matheson's kisses could certainly be dangerous, perhaps even downright deadly.

* * * *

Jamie's skin hunger for more contact with Bella rode him hard. One kiss was all he needed to ensure he'd embedded his scent into her again, but as she buried her hands in his hair, he fought the bone-deep need he had to topple her to the ground and stake his claim more fully. Every inch of him had battled at allowing her to remain so close to those rogues as she'd administered the sedative, no matter they were out of it. Being males from an offshoot clan meant they certainly posed a threat. A big threat since they had no allegiance to their chief or clan.

"Can't breathe," she gasped against his lips.

"Too bad." With single-minded determination, he explored her deeper, his grip on her chin and the back of her head firm so he could ensure her face remained at just the right angle for him to catch every delicious moan currently escaping her lips. He gave her his breath before gentling his touch and finding what he needed inside of himself to pull back. Not far. Just an inch. Her luscious pink lips were kiss-swollen and his scent surrounded her. Perfect, well, almost perfect. He shrugged his denim jacket off and slung it around her shoulders. "Arms in."

Breath hitching, she shoved her arms down the sleeves then pulled the front sides of his jacket together. "I never knew you could be so territorial. Is this better?"

"Almost." He zipped his jacket up and encased her completely in his scent. Only then did a little more of his usual calm settle into place. "That's about as good as it's going to get for now."

"May I go?"

"Make it there and back as quick as you can, and don't touch either operative when they arrive, not even to shake their hands."

"Wait." She frowned something fierce, her nose pinching at the brow and the tiny mole beside one corner of her mouth drawing inward. "You're going too far with that request."

"Aye, I am." Yet he couldn't have stopped himself from issuing that command even if he'd tried. Perhaps he still needed to instill even more space between them. Aye, that might help clear his muddled mind. He backed away from her another three feet, the distance he now inflicted riling his bear and making him claw for release. They both wanted her back, and preferably within touching range. "Go, before I say anything else that might upset you."

"I will shake their hands if I please," she huffed as she backed up then turned around. She strode back along the scrub-lined trail they'd not long traversed, her blond locks now messed although still swaying so damn enticingly to her lush backside. The pale strands caught the late afternoon sunshine speckling through the canopy overhead and glimmered a silky golden hue.

He'd not long ago had his hands in her hair, her body molded to his and naught had ever felt so right. Her bear had also exploded forth when the rogues had arrived and she'd been drawn into aiding him and when she had, those come-and-get-me pheromones she'd emitted had been three-times stronger than ever before. Her bear might still be another month shy of full maturity, but had she been at Matheson Castle when she'd made that Change, she'd have drawn every single one of the thirty-seven unmated males into a power play in order to nab her attention.

She was beyond ripe for the taking, and he shuddered to think how much riper her intoxicating scent would be in the weeks ahead. Aye, it would be sheer hell being contained within the same walls as her until the next full moon rose.

He wanted her. His bear wanted her.

And if she was mated to another man, then his heart would surely be crushed in two.

He shook his head, tried to clear it of those unhelpful thoughts. He'd have to wait just as the rest of the men waited. No other choice.

Claws extended, he slammed them into the closest trunk and ripped downward. He scoured the rough bark, over and over until the *whop-whop* of blades cut through the air above and the droning sound of a chopper flew toward the B&B. Manning and Sutherland were here.

Pacing the trail in front of the downed rogues, the men trapped in their bear form until they awoke when the effects of the sedative wore off, he kept one eye alert on them and the other on the trail Bella would soon appear along.

A pretty whistle tinkled through the trees. Bella. He'd never mistake her call. She approached with the operatives and a flight-suited pilot, her warning of her coming arrival one he heeded.

Teeth gritted, he planted himself in the middle of the trail, and as she stepped up to him, her hands stuffed in the pockets of his battered denim jacket and the collar lifted around her neck, he wrapped an arm around her waist and tucked her in behind him. With his gaze on the operatives carrying two stretchers between them, he said, "Did you all have a good flight?"

"We were already close, so it was swift," Manning answered, the tallest of the three. He set one stretcher down before the first bear, while Sutherland and the pilot, Gunner, who he'd met before set their stretcher down before the second rogue. "How long will the sedation last?" Manning asked him.

"Twelve hours."

With his black hair razored close to his scalp, Manning nodded his approval. "On our fly-over in we spotted a dinged-up, mustard-colored truck parked under an oak in the forest about two miles to the direct north of this spot, just off the road along a gravel track. I've called in another team, but with how remote this place is, they might take an hour to get here. I'd say it belongs to these two.

"I'll take a look at the vehicle and the location as soon as we get back." He'd need to scout the area out before too many others marked it with their scents and tracks.

"Sure, understood. I'll radio that through, for them to approach with care. Let's get these two back to the chopper and loaded." Manning nodded to Sutherland and Gunner. "Load 'em up and let's go."

The other two men hoisted one bear onto their stretcher, and he joined Manning and helped him haul the second bear onto the second stretcher. Gunner and Sutherland headed out first and he and Manning followed, Bella right on his rear.

She fiddled with her earrings, slotted the dangling gold chain of one back more firmly in place then brushed past him and took the lead as she walked ahead of their group.

With her heavenly aroma wafting to him on the breeze, he tried to corral his thoughts and keep his mind on Manning as the operative continued to fire out questions pertaining to all that had happened leading up to and including the rogues' capture. These operatives were amongst a small and elite team of men who were aware of what their clansmen could do, although he kept any talk of Bella's shift from the discussion as he outlined the rundown.

Finally, they emerged from the forest and entered the clearing at the rear of the inn, the skies darkening overhead and lights now blazing from within the windows of the lower floor of the B&B. Smoke puffed from the chimney, curled into the air and swirled away on the wind.

Gordon stepped out from the rear paneled door and glared at the bears they carried. "I hope that's it."

"Only two bears were reported missing from the park. That I can assure you," Manning told Gordon. "You, your wife, and any future guests can return to these woods as soon as you please."

"That's good to know. Thank you for all that you've done." Gordon clapped the operative on the back then gripped Jamie's shoulder. "Greer and I will sleep more soundly knowing this threat is now gone."

"Bella and I will remain here for the night as scheduled, but first we're going to check out a spot where these two might have been earlier, ensure all is clear then return." He and Manning slid their stretcher inside the chopper before backing out of the way so Gunner and Sutherland could do the same with theirs.

Bears loaded, Gunner jogged around to the cockpit and eased in behind the controls. Manning and Sutherland boarded and closed the side door with a *clunk*. The blades whirred and the chopper lifted.

Wind blasted all around as he backed up and joined Bella where she already waited a safer distance away. The lush grass swayed in pulsating circles outward and the branches of the closest trees breezed back and forth while the horses snickered from within the corral. Gordon left them and opened the corral gate and led his mares into the stables where they'd remain secure for the night.

"You ready to go?" Bella nudged his arm with her arm, her cheeks all flushed from their excursion, likely flushed from excitement too. There was naught more rewarding than catching a rogue or two.

"Sure am."

"I sent the chief a text as we walked back and messaged him that we're headed to the rogues' vehicle. I sent him a pic of the bears once you'd loaded them into the chopper. He'll enjoy the update, I'm sure."

"Good job." He set a hand at the small of her back and ushered her along the rear walkway around the B&B and across the graveled parking lot. SUV passenger door opened, he gestured her inside and once she'd seated herself, he closed her door and jogged around to his own. As she clicked her belt into place, he backed out and with a squeal of the tires, took off due north in the direction Manning had given him.

Two miles along the crumbly-edged blacktop, he stopped where a stony, grass-matted side track led off into the forest, a trail half obscured by the woods surrounding it. "This must be the place. We'll walk from here."

"I can make out tire tracks." She pointed to the two flattened lines of grass. "I'm wondering how often the rogues might have used this trail. It would take a few trips in and out to embed those kinds of deeper score marks into the grass."

"We'll soon find out." He marched around the rear of the vehicle while she hopped out and unzipped his jacket. "No." He nabbed her hands, zipped her back up and arched a brow. "Keep it on."

"You sure?"

"I'm running hotter than usual, so aye." He also needed to see her in it, like with a gut-deep need. "Those rogues also shifted both yesterday and again today, which makes two days in a row, something few of the shifters within the weakened bloodlines can do." Their blood had also smelt off, as it could do when an ailment had struck them. "They're not right in some way."

"I agree, and since they tried to attack both Gordon and Greer, as well as us without any provocation, there's definitely something wrong."

Bears were hunters, but their kind only attacked when first threatened. Neither he or Bella had done that, and he could guarantee that Gordon and Greer hadn't either.

He walked toward the trail, the sky darkening further as the sun settled low on the horizon. Along the path, he marched, the cooler evening breeze washing over him. Lugging in a deep breath, he continued on, the deep earthiness of the land calling to his very soul, just as the woman at his side did.

"You got something already?" She hooked one finger into the belt loop of his black pants and gave it a tug. "You're walking real fast."

"Aye, because I've got a fierce urge to bite you."

"Mmm, that sounds promising." She giggled, the sweet

musical tinkle searing him deep inside his soul.

"Stay back from me for a bit, all right?" Picking up his pace, he bounded over snaking tree roots and ducked his head under the odd low branch then bingo. A small clearing opened up with a majestic oak tree gracing the center of it. Underneath the wide bough of the tree, one mustard-colored truck sat half hidden underneath it, the hood poking out. "It was lucky Manning spotted this."

"Luck seems to be on our side today." Bella stole past him and with a critical eye, surveyed the truck as she walked around it. At the rear, she flipped the canvas cover off the deck and whistled at the sight of a cooking-burner and chiller bins holding what must surely be food. "They've either been camping out for a while, or intended to."

"Let's hope they also intended on camping out with ID in the vehicle." The number plates had been removed. Not a good sign. He cranked open the front door of the truck, thankfully unlocked, and flipped open the glove compartment. A handgun and a case of bullets sat nestled amongst food wrappers galore. His bear growled low and hard, the vibration a deep rattle in his chest. "They also better have a license for carrying this weapon too."

"I've got some personal belongings here." From the back seat, she hauled out two dirty and torn duffel bags and set them on the damp grass. She crouched and he hunkered down and joined her. "You want me to do the honors?"

"Sure." He caught a long shaft of her hair and ran his fingers down the silky length. As he did, she flipped open the flap of the first duffel and plucked a wallet from the top. She opened it, turned it toward him and showed him the driver's license nestled safely in the front pouch behind a clear plastic covering. The name Logan Gabriel Matthews was emblazoned on the card, along with a picture of a young man with dark hair and silver-rimmed round glasses.

"Matthews is definitely a sept of clan Matheson," she murmured low and all sexy.

"Aye, the son of Matthew we are." He motioned to the bags. "Keep going."

She set the wallet on the grass, turned the first duffle upside-down and jiggled it, then the second. A tumble of clothes fell into a heap, along with an assortment of knives and an envelope with a medical center's emblem printed on one corner. "Should I take a look inside?"

"Go for it." He shuffled closer, curled his body more fully around hers to ward off the chilly breeze blowing through.

She opened the envelope, the sticky flap loose from being opened before. Papers unfolded, she scanned the words by the dimming daylight and he did so as well. They were test results from a doctor's office in Inverness, pertaining to Logan and Heylin Matthews, age twenty-seven, twin brothers, both being treated for stage four—

"Oh, they have prostate cancer." Bella lowered the papers and eyed him over her shoulder.

"Keep reading."

"Sure." Papers lifted again, she traced one finger along the first paragraph and read the words embedded there, "As discussed, unfortunately this is the last stage of prostate cancer. The tumors have spread to other parts of your bodies, including the lungs, liver, bones, and lymph nodes. I realize this information is bleak, although keep in mind every case is different and with the advancements in prostate cancer treatment, there is still more we can do. I need to see you both in my offices as soon as possible. Call and make a time immediately. We'll begin treatment as soon as a plan is laid out for you both." She eased back a little on her knees, her back sliding right up against his chest as she half-turned into him. "They're both so very ill."

"We'll need to hand this letter on to both Manning and the chief, ensure they're made aware of this news." At least Logan and Heylin hadn't in truth harmed Gordon and Greer. Sure, they'd kept them stuck in a tree for hours on end, but they hadn't actually drawn blood. Neither had they gotten their teeth into him or Bella. Sinking his hand even deeper into her glorious blond locks, he muttered, "When a shifter is unwell, fresh and healthy shifter blood is needed to be infused with ours to increase our natural ability to heal. Liam will be able to aid them better than any human doctor could."

"Liam would be up for it too. What they did to Gordon and Greer was wrong, but they didn't go beyond the point of no return. There's still hope for them."

"Liam's also perfected shifter blood transfusions of late. He has a good amount of blood from the two strongest shifter lines in stock, both from Ivanson Castle and our own keep." He stroked down her back. "Our resident doctor needs to see this letter. Take a picture of this and the license and send it all through to both him and the chief."

"Will do." She snapped the pictures needed and fired them away.

He lifted his nose and caught the distinct musk of human males, three separate notes belonging to three separate men. Rising, he stood firmly in front of Bella and waited for the coming men to arrive.

"Try and relax." From behind him, she slid her hand under his t-shirt and hooked it around his waist, her forearm firm against his belly and her nose pressed to his back. Quietly, she murmured, "The full moon is now rising and escalating your emotions. Your barriers are down by the way, all the way down."

"I need to get you out of here." He wasn't going to haul his shields back up, not when she'd moved so quickly to touch him after sensing his riled emotions. That he needed, to the depths of his very soul.

"They're not bears, only you are. You shouldn't be this worried." She slid her fingers just under the front fastening of his pants, his shirt thankfully hiding sight of what she did and her extremely possessive touch calming him as nothing else could.

"I'm not wearing any underwear, Bella, so lower your hand any further and you're going to encounter hard flesh."

"Is that right?" A teasing answer as she lifted her hand back out and spread her fingers wide across his abs. She petted him, each of her slow and satisfying strokes keeping the snarl he wished to release from bursting free of his lips.

"You better damn well be mine." Soft words that went no further than her, the stillness of the night broken only by the footsteps of the men as they closed in. So close now.

"I hope you're mine as well." She scraped her fingers gently along his skin, her warm breath fanning his back through his shirt. "Have I ever told you I want lots of cubs?"

"I'm not surprised you do."

"Do you want lots of cubs too?" Such husky words, like a siren's call to both him and his bear.

"Aye, as many as my mate is willing to give me."

"Does half a dozen sound a little overwhelming?" She scraped her fingers up his chest and across his flat nipples, which for some reason stiffened them, and who the hell knew they'd be that sensitive to a woman's touch. "I'm going to want my mate to bed me often, and keep me satisfied in the most elemental way. A lot of cubs are going to come from that kind of love."

"That doesn't sound overwhelming at all, and rein in all the sexy talk. I'm getting as hard as a damn spike." She was going to send him insane for sure, then he'd be bringing out the claws when the operatives arrived and tearing into them. They'd only have to look at her the wrong way and he'd bare their blood.

"It's the full moon's fault. I'm never this chatty, frisky and needy all at once." She rubbed against his back, her breasts poking into his shirt and her own nipples just as stiff as his since they scraped so sensually against him.

"Back up a little, Bella." Only the men broke free of the

trees with torches in hand, and he snagged her arms wrapped around him and kept her firmly at his back. Overhead, the skies had gone completely black, and attired in camouflage pants and black muscle tees with their weapons slung over their shoulders, the men strode directly toward him.

The man at the head, clearly the leader, nodded at him. "Manning informed us you'd be here. I'm Guy MacDonald. Find anything of interest during your search?"

"We certainly did." Bella snuck her arms out of his tight hold and eased out from behind him. She handed the evidence they'd collected across to MacDonald. "I've already sent pictures of this license and the letter to my chief, as well as to our clan doctor. The two men in question are Logan and Heylin Matthews, twin brothers aged twenty-seven, and both being treated for stage four prostate cancer."

"We'll liaise with your chief and share any new information directly with him if and when it comes to hand." MacDonald motioned for the other two operatives with him to search the vehicle. "You have our thanks for capturing the rogues."

"It's all part of a day's work," he answered for both him and Bella, and with his bear fairly tearing him up inside—his need to get Bella away from these men riding him hard—he steered her swiftly away from the operatives and back along the trail. Hell, he really shouldn't be in this much of a mess, his emotions so on edge, but kissing her earlier and smothering her in his scent had heightened his feral need for her all the more.

"I can sense you're riding the edge, so whatever you need simply state it." She ducked under a low branch, a strand of her hair snagging on it and fluttering free.

He snatched the strand out of the air before it could wisp away on the breeze and tucked it into his pocket without her thankfully noticing. "Keeping you away from any men I consider a threat is all that's needed."

"Well, you're doing a fine job of that already." She strode

ahead and the moon's golden light bathed her in its ethereal glow and made his heart clench in on itself.

One in thirty-seven, he mumbled to himself. *There's only the minutest chance she's yours.*

"How about we both shift together later tonight? You can have me all to yourself in the woods." She glanced at him over her shoulder, her lips lifting in a mischievousness smile. "I haven't had the chance to let my bear out for a proper play yet, and she desperately wishes to have some fun, and preferably with you."

"Since the rogues have been caught"—he patted the last vial of sedative secured in his pocket—"I'm going to stick to my earlier plan and have an early night. You'll have to shift alone." There wasn't a chance he'd take the risk of shifting with her in his current mood. He'd also—since she'd moved into the room across from his chamber—taken his fair share of sedatives over the years and tonight a sedative was definitely needed.

"Scaredy-cat."

"I'm a bear, not a cat, and my beast toppled you to the ground earlier. If it weren't for the rogues turning up, he might very well have tried to have his wicked way with you." They broke free of the tree line and he escorted her to the passenger's side, closed the door after she'd seated herself then came around and slid behind the wheel.

The short drive back took no time at all and once he'd parked in the lot and turned the ignition off, he faced her. "I apologize for being rough earlier." Possessive was more like it. "Do you forgive me?"

"I honestly didn't mind you being a little rough." She wriggled around and faced him, the richness of the black leather interior surrounding her. "In all truth, I may have even liked it."

"We clearly need to step back from each other for a bit, insert some space so to speak." He couldn't push her about like that again. She was a woman and deserved to be treated with respect and reverence.

"We're kin, pack, and the best of friends." She reached out a hand and cupped his jaw. Gently, she stroked her fingers back and forth along his cheek then trailed one fingertip along his lower lip.

"Your touch is so incredibly mesmerizing." He desperately wanted more of it.

"Touching as we've done today is necessary for shifters."

"Kissing isn't."

"It is between mates, and you never know, you might be mine." Smiling, she unzipped his jacket and shrugged it off. Passing it to him, she murmured, "Thanks for the loan of this. Let's go eat. I'm famished."

"You forgive far too quickly."

"Like I already said, I truly didn't mind your roughness." She pushed her door open, closed it with a *clunk* then sauntered toward the front door of the B&B.

He locked the SUV and marched after her. Sliding his jacket on, he got immersed in her heavenly lily scent and his bear rolled around within him at the decadent pleasure. Absolutely perfect, yet also absolutely intolerable. His heart twisted painfully inside his chest.

What he wouldn't give to ensure she was his.

One in an agonizing thirty-seven weren't the best of odds.

Those he could never forget.

Chapter 4

Sailing along Loch Alsh, 1211.

As Annabella and Jamie sailed along Loch Alsh toward the underground caves near the headland, Annabella stood plastered against him, her lips a mere breath from his as she awaited his answer. "Please kiss me, Jamie. Dinnae deny me any longer."

"I wish to kiss you, but should I start, I willnae wish to stop." His arms banded tighter around her, his hold so deliciously firm.

Never had another warrior from their fae village ever instilled this kind of desire within her, and even before they'd discovered their mated bond had taken form on the last full moon, she'd still known without a doubt that he was hers. Looking deep into his eyes, she wanted only to drown in the dark shimmering depths. "I have no issue if you dinnae wish to stop."

"We arena anticipating our wedding night, if that's what you're asking. One more fortnight. That's all we must wait."

"You are far too stubborn for your own good."

"One of us must—hold on." A large wave loomed and he held onto both her and the ropes as they sailed over the foamy white crest then came down hard on the other side.

Spray washed over the sides and she barely kept her feet under her. She surely would've fallen overboard if she hadn't been holding onto her chosen one and he holding onto her. "Dinnae let go of me."

"I'll never let go of you, and we're almost at the beach which leads to the inland caves you wish to visit."

Up ahead, a white sand beach curved around a bay surrounded by a jagged rock wall and a river gushing into the swirling incoming tide to one side. "Have you explored the caves afore?"

"Aye, the main cavern holds a pool of hot water."

"Oh, I'd dearly love a swim."

"If you wish, you may." Jamie adjusted the angle of the sail and sent them cruising toward land. As his skiff skirted the waves rolling into shore, he dropped the sail then bounded into the knee-deep water and heaved the boat half up onto the sand. He held out his arms to her where the surf crashed in. "Jump. There's no need for you to get wet."

"As you wish." She'd adored having his arms around her as they'd sailed, detested it when he'd let her go. She jumped and he caught her with a chuckle and swung her onto the dry sand before securing his skiff to a boulder with the mooring rope.

With the wind plastering his billowy white shirt to his wide chest, his muscles bunching and his dark hair breezing about, he joined her and caught her hands, and for the first time in a very long time, his natural fae shields within his mind fully lowered. His emotions pulsed free and she couldn't help but grab ahold of them and dissect each one.

He wanted her, and with a depth of need he'd never allowed her to see before.

It was a need which reverberated just as strongly within her.

She wanted to complete their bond this very night, when the full moon rose, not to wait until they spoke vows in a fortnight's time, and for some strange reason she feared if she allowed either of them to wait that length of time, it might very well be the worst mistake they ever made.

She needed to seduce him this day, by whatever means she could.

Aye, she wanted her mate, for them to be as one, from this day forth.

Chapter 5

Bella thanked Greer for the delicious dinner meal. The roast beef had been cooked to perfection, the sautéed potatoes and buttered carrots mouthwatering. Still, she had so much she wished to do this night, including relaxing in the bath before shifting in order to appease her inner bear.

She pushed her chair back from the dining table, the meal having been a celebration of sorts now the rogue bears had been taken away. "Thank you for the meal, Greer. It was delicious as usual."

"You're most welcome." Smiling, Greer sipped her tea, while Gordon stirred sugar in his coffee, the bay window overlooking the clearing beyond the dining room bathed in golden moonlight.

She moved in behind Jamie and squeezed his shoulders. "Sleep well. Don't let the bed bugs bite."

"There'll be no bed bugs biting me, or for that matter any other animals." He covered one of her hands on his shoulder, his guilt at his sheer dominance of earlier rolling off him.

"Then you'd best keep your door locked if you want the other animals to remain out." Teasing words she murmured in his ear, and since she couldn't help herself, she popped a kiss on the top of his head, the affectionate touch one he needed and the soft rumble he emitted, clear proof as well. Aye, he might feel bad about what had happened earlier between them, but Jamie had always intrigued her, made her heart beat faster and even though she'd never truly acted upon those desires until now, she couldn't help but want more with him. One in thirty-seven. Surely the odds were better than that considering the intense feelings she'd always had for him. Whether he was near or not, he'd always consumed her mind.

With another quick squeeze of his shoulder, she left him behind and trod upstairs, opened his bedroom door instead of hers and snuck one of his t-shirts from his duffel—the marbled gray cotton one. It was his favorite, slightly worn along the cuffs and hem, but it held his scent even though it had been washed before he'd packed it. Certainly after wearing his jacket and having to hand it back, she'd missed being wrapped up in his scent. His heavenly aroma was like a drug. Once taken in, quickly desired again, and the best remedy to keep that addiction at bay was to have his scent on her since the man had no intention of providing that himself.

She wandered into the bathroom joining their rooms, flicked the lock on the door on his side then stuffed his shirt under her nose and breathed in his mind-shattering scent a second time. So warm and spicy, the sweetest allure she wanted more of.

We clearly need to step back from each other for a bit, insert some space so to speak.

Not happening. She wouldn't allow it, only now she needed to figure out a way to ensure he understood that too. She wanted more with him, no matter she was still a month shy of her bear's full maturity.

In the bathroom, she set his t-shirt on the vanity, plugged the bath and dribbled lily bubble bath under the steady stream of hot water pouring from the spout. Boots kicked off and jeans and tank top stripped away, she sank into the luxurious water, the bubbles a decadent foam around her neck.

How was she to make certain he couldn't step away from her, and insert that space he wanted to? Seduce him perhaps? Hmm, she was totally up for that, and she did have her current location to her advantage. He certainly couldn't run away from her here, or at least not as easily as he could once they returned to Matheson Castle.

Through the window above the vanity, moonlight beamed in and she raised her bubbly hands and played them through the air, the light reflecting off in sparkly bursts. There was nothing more beautiful than a full moon and its heady draw. Aye, she most definitely had her current location and this one magical night in which to lure him to her.

"Bella?" Jamie's grumpy voice rasped through the door. "You've been in my room. Why?"

"I pinched one of your shirts." She cleared her throat. "I missed having your scent on me."

"I see." He cleared his own throat, then went strangely quiet.

With a deep fortifying breath, she focused her skill on the man standing on the other side of the door. "Do you want to join me in the bath? It's plenty big enough for two and I know you can pick that lock in a second. I'm also fairly decent since I'm covered in a mound of bubbles."

A wave of heated need flared through to her, although just as swiftly as it had escaped him, he tightened his barriers and locked those emotions promptly off. Still, she'd most certainly made a dent in his all-important armor. She'd try it again.

"Jamie." His name came out all breathy, and not on purpose. "I dare you to join me."

"You should never dare one who holds the 'power of thought,' Annabella."

"Don't call me Annabella in that angry way. I've warned

you—" A flurry of images shimmered before her eyes and she gasped.

Jamie stood upon the sea-gate landing of Matheson Castle dressed in black battle leathers and a loose white tunic, her Jamie, yet not her Jamie. There was something slightly different about him. His clothing for certain, and their surroundings. Matheson Castle didn't appear quite the same as it did now, but more like the picture of their keep which hung in Murdock's office, one their chief and seer had drawn from a vision he'd had of their fae-shifter clan from the twelve-hundreds. Before her, Jamie released the mooring rope of a skiff, one similar in design to those built centuries ago, then with a swift hand, he coiled and tossed the rope into the center of the hull before glancing over his shoulder at her. Nay, not at her, but at a woman behind her with blond hair. The woman wore a gown with red woolen skirts that beat against her legs in the brisk sea breeze, a woman who looked strikingly similar to her, right down to the mole next to the corner of her mouth. What on earth was going on?

The identical woman planted her hands on hips as she stood stoically facing the man who looked like her Jamie. "Jamie, we're mated, betrothed and soon to be wed, but you seem so intent on no' spending any further time with me between now and our wedding day. I'm an empath. I can sense your emotions and your frustration smothers me."

Clutching a hand to her mouth, she flung her gaze between the two people who appeared to be in the middle of an argument.

"Kissing is for wedded couples, Annabella. We have another fourteen days until we speak vows. I willnae bring any dishonor down upon your head by taking more from you than I currently should." He jabbed a finger at the keep rising high behind her. "Back inside with you now."

"I won the wager between us last eve," the woman continued, "and you promised me that if I did you'd take me to the caves farther along the loch. I long to see the place which your parents so often speak about, and the only way there is if I tread across the boggy marshland, which I've no intention of doing, no' when you're already sailing alongside the coastline in that direction. Please, take me."

"Your brother willnae permit any man to be alone with you, and night will soon fall. 'Tis only a mere few hours away."

"Do you see my brother here right now?" She waved a hand around the landing devoid of even one soul. "My brother's ridden out for the headland to take over the point watchman's duty and willnae return until the morrow. Now is the only time I can go. Please." She laid a hand on his arm. "Will you no' keep your word?"

"I always keep my word." Gritting his teeth, he gestured to his skiff. "In with you now then, afore I change my mind."

"Thank you." With a grin of success, the woman swished past him, clambered on board and eased onto the bench seat at the stern.

"Bella?" A thump rattled the door. "Are you all right?"

"I'm not sure." She splashed upright in the bath. What the hell had that vision been all about?

A low growl rumbled back at her then she lifted up out of the water—and not of her own accord. Jamie lifted her using his telekinesis and through the door no less. She'd never seen him perform such a feat. "Put me down, Jamie."

"I need to come in there and make certain you're all right. I can't do that while you're in the bath." He swung her upright and settled her on her feet next to the vanity. "Get dressed, now."

"Okay." She snagged a fluffy white towel and rubbed herself dry, then tugged Jamie's gray t-shirt on which swamped her to her knees. The rounded neckline slid half off one of her shoulders, but she was decent enough. "Come in."

The lock clicked open on her side, by use of his skill, then he shoved the door open and scooped her up against him. "Some strange vision just assailed me, then you wouldn't answer me when I called out."

"I had a vision too. A myriad of images, of a man and woman just like you and me, with the same names as us. They were talking, or fighting, or something like that, right at the sea-gate landing of Matheson Castle."

"That's exactly what I saw too. A flurry of images from sometime back in the twelve-hundreds clouded my sight. I couldn't pinpoint the exact time, but the sea-gate landing is located farther to the right where it is now and Murdock has an image of it sketched and hanging in his solar. He drew them from a vision he'd had in his youth."

"What does all this mean, and why did we both see the same vision?" Delayed shock coursed through her, making her legs shake.

"I've no idea." He rubbed her back, his heat penetrating through and warming her. "Let's get you into bed. You've had quite the fright."

Numb, she allowed him to steer her into her bedroom.

He flicked off the bathroom light and closed the door, pulled the white-quilted comforter back and motioned for her to slide between the sheets. With naught but the moonlight shimmering through the white net curtains over the window, she rubbed her arms while he hovered over her.

She wasn't a child who needed protecting from bad dreams, but neither could she pass up this opportunity since he appeared hesitant to leave. She patted the space beside her, and he plopped down. "I haven't had a chance to shift yet."

"It's best you don't considering what just happened. It wouldn't hurt for either of us to hit the sack early." He removed the last remaining vial from his pocket and held it up. "I need to take this."

"Will you take it here, and lie beside me for the night? I don't want to be alone right now, not after that vision."

He stared at her, his golden shifter eyes darkening, then he slowly nodded. "Sure, I can do that."

"Thank you."

"Give me a minute." He walked out the door, but returned less than thirty seconds later wearing black silk boxers. He climbed into bed beside her, his heavily muscled chest on glorious display and his abs rippling so deliciously close. With the covers bunched at his waist, he gritted his teeth. "I'll be here, in body if not in mind. Seek whatever comfort you need from me while I'm out of it."

"You truly don't mind if I do?"

"No, not after that vision we both had." He handed her the vial.

She uncapped it, slid one hand under his head on the pillow and tipped the orange concoction between his lips.

He gulped the sedative down, caught her face between his hands and stroked his thumbs across her cheeks. "You can keep my shirt, or at least until the next full moon rises." His indecently long eyelashes fluttered down, his voice slurring as he forced them back up again. "Afffterrr that"—his tongue got all sloppy—"y-your mate will want-ta-you in his sh-sh—"

"Shirt, I know." She pressed one finger to his lips. "And I hope that mate is you."

"So the h-hell-o do I."

She giggled. "Good night, Jamie."

"N-night. His hands slipped from her cheeks and dropped to his sides, then his head slumped.

Huh, how frustrating. The sedative had kicked in far too fast for her liking.

Grumbling under her breath, she popped a kiss on the tip of his nose, pulled the covers over them both and with her cheek nestled on his chest, traced along the razz of stubble gracing his jaw, the cleft in his chin so damn sexy. The most delicious dimples sat either side of his full lips, his long sooty lashes sweeping his high cheeks.

Gently, she lifted one of his heavy hands and threaded her fingers through his, and only once she was connected so strongly to him, did she close her own eyes and allow the dark of the night to claim her too.

* * * *

Outside, a rooster crowed and the horses whinnied within the corral. Bella stretched and opened her eyes, blinked at the morning sunshine streaming through the nets and smiled as sheer satisfaction thrummed through her. Best. Sleep. Ever.

She wriggled one leg fully over both of Jamie's legs, her cheek still on his wide chest where she'd rested it last night. Likely he'd still be completely out of it for another couple of hours since the sedative always lasted a full twelve hours.

Seek whatever comfort you need from me while I'm out of it.

She'd definitely sought that comfort, hopefully offered some of her own in return even though he hadn't been awake at the time.

Beep, beep.

She lifted her head at the intrusion. Her cell phone beeped from somewhere in the bathroom, likely still inside the pocket of her jeans. Out of bed, she heaved, collected her annoying phone then returned to the bed, settled in beside Jamie again and flicked the screen to the incoming message.

One more month for you. XO

She smiled at Isla's message and fired off a return to her dearest friend. *I'm in bed with Jamie.*

An answering ring, and not a text message. She pressed the answer button, got a, "What?" screeched in her ear.

"We're on a mission, caught a couple of rogue bears last night at the MacDonald's B&B."

"That's not what I meant by 'what?' Spill. Now." A buzz of voices echoed in the background and the *tap-tap* of Isla's shoes across a hard floor resounded.

"Where are you?"

"Back at Matheson Castle with my mate. Iain and I are about to have breakfast in the great hall. I couldn't find you to have a catch-up, then Dad informed me that you and Jamie were on a mission so I fired off the message. What are you doing in bed with him?"

"We kissed yesterday, and wow, I definitely liked it. We also both got a shock when we had a joint vision last night, one of two people who looked exactly like us but who lived in ancient times. They even had our names. The woman, Annabella, said they were mated and betrothed. She was an empath too." She rolled into Jamie and tucked her leg back over his legs, the crisp hairs on his lower limbs tickling her skin.

"Since when did you and Jamie start having joint visions?"

"That was the first one. I'd like to talk to the chief about it."

"That's a good idea. You should also know that Hunter is back from his mission and eager to catch up with you. He's outside training at the moment, and releasing some frustration along with it. I'm not sure what's upsetting him, but he's in a foul mood today."

"He's been struggling on the night of each full moon, what with his senses roaring so strong. He wants to find his mate, and don't tell him about this conversation. He'll be even more frustrated if he hears Jamie and I have kissed."

"So will all the other unmated males."

"I'll call Hunter now and let him know I'm okay. That might help ease a little of his frustration." She and her brother were close, rarely kept anything from each other, although in regards to what had just happened between her and Jamie, that wouldn't be going any further than them.

"I'll chat to you when you get back."

"Talk to you soon." She hung up and jabbed in Hunter's number and smiled when he answered with a grunt and the clear clanging of swords in the background. "And good morning to you too."

"The chief said you and Jamie caught two rogue bears last night on your mission. One second." Steel reverberated loud against steel, although became more muted as his footsteps scuffed the ground. He must be leaving the training area. "Just finding a quieter spot."

"Thanks, and that's right. We caught two rogues by the name of Logan and Heylin Matthews, twin brothers aged twenty-seven, and both being treated for stage four prostate cancer. Jamie and I found their vehicle in the woods."

"The chief told me that as well. You should know that Murdock's already sent Liam out to their confinement location to see them." He cleared his throat. "I really need to speak to Jamie. I sent him a message but he hasn't responded yet."

"The full moon wasn't easy on him and he sedated himself."

"The unmated men here are all on edge, which is increasing my own edginess. They didn't care having you so far away last night."

"They would have found it harder had I been there."

"Aye." He snorted under his breath. "Did Jamie behave himself last night?"

"You wouldn't have agreed with the chief we could partner up if you'd thought he wouldn't." She ran her fingers through Jamie's dark brown hair wisped with black strands and the odd golden one. "When he wakes up, I'll have him—"

Jamie groaned and twitched his legs under hers.

"Ah, I've got to go. He's waking up."

"What do you mean he's waking up?"

"I popped into his room to check on him. Love you. Talk to you when I get back." She powered off her cell phone and tossed it on the bedside table where it landed with a *thud*.

"Bella?" Jamie murmured her name as he rolled into her, his hand sliding over her hip and around to her bottom.

"I'm here." She stroked the back of his head.

"I heard you talking to someone. Who was it?" His fingers slid underneath the cotton of her borrowed shirt and up her back, his eyes sluggishly opening.

"I spoke to Isla first then Hunter. The chief updated Hunter on our case and Liam's already left to see Logan and Heylin Matthews."

"Good. I have a feeling there's something we might be able to do to help them." His fingers trailed around to the front, his knuckles brushing the undersides of her breasts and with his warm breath feathering across her lips, he smiled at her. "I like waking up next to you."

"I liked it too, and that you're touching me so freely."

"Your bear's fairly purring inside of you. I can hear her." He circled one of her breasts with his fingertips then cupped the mound fully in his palm and made her gasp at the wonderful shock of it.

Jamie was touching her bare skin, her breasts and nipples too. Nothing could have made her happier. Aye, waking up with him still so drowsy from the sedative he'd taken was good, real good.

"My bear's always liked your touch." She gripped the hem of her shirt, hoisted it over her head and tossed it aside. "She wants to come out and play, doesn't want to wait any longer and since you clearly seem to be in the right mood, she wants to do that with you right now, this very second."

Jamie grabbed in a breath, his throat working as his gaze slid to her breasts then shot back to her eyes. "You should have warned me you were about to do that. Us being naked around each other is dangerous."

"I like danger, and you're still wearing boxers. I also want you to shift with me, in case you didn't catch that."

"If I get too rough, put me back in my place." He slid out of bed, taking her with him, his hands on her waist as he set her on her feet with her back against the wall. Thumbs in the waistband of his black boxes, he pushed them down his muscled legs and kicked them away then with his hands planted on the wall either side of her head, he caged her in with his body. "You ready to shift?"

"Embed your scent into me first." She tried heartedly hard to keep her gaze on his and not to wander down toward the stiffness of his erection currently jabbing into her belly.

"You're already smothered in it, which has completely soothed and yet also aggravated my bear." He dipped his head to hers. "You're like a seductive siren."

"Aye, and it appears I'm your siren. I want you to bite me." She rubbed her breasts against his rock-hard chest, stuck her nose in his neck and nuzzled his skin and as she did, she tipped her neck to the side in offering. "Please, Jamie."

"Now is not the time for this kind of, ah, play." His claws sliced out and he stabbed them into the white painted wall and held perfectly still. "Make the Change before I lose all thought and truly do try to bite you."

"I've never asked any man to bite me, other than you." Stroking the bulging muscles of his arms, she caressed from his wrists to his biceps. "I want you to sink your teeth into me, the same time as I sink my teeth into you."

"Ah, hell." He scoured the wall, claws slicing downward then with an intensely raw growl, cupped both her breasts, lifted them higher and head dipped, licked one nipple.

The hot rasp of his tongue across the sensitive bud sent a flurry of need pulsing straight to her core. She dragged in a deep breath, dust flaking from the score marks he'd made fluttering to the floor. "How are you going to explain that damage?"

"I've no idea." He licked her other nipple. "But I do know your brother is going to beat me black and blue for having touched you like this, and I'm not going to stop him when I clearly deserve everything coming to me. I shouldn't be touching you at all."

"I don't intend on telling my brother about our time here, and you're not going to tell him either. I'll also shower before we leave, make sure there isn't a trace of your scent on me, that way neither he or any of our kin will pick up anything. You do the same and rid yourself of my scent, and we'll be fine."

"You are making far more sense than you should." With a snarl and a snap of his teeth, he sank them into the upper curve of her breast, not hard enough to break her skin, but definitely hard enough to leave his mark.

"Bite me again." She tapped her neck. "You know where I truly want it."

His golden shifter eyes turned a feral hue. "I can't give you the claiming mark, no matter how much I want to."

He was right. He couldn't. And she should stop pushing him, only she seemed to have lost her mind completely.

"Make the Change now." He backed up one step.

"All right." It was best if she did. She dropped to all fours and for a mere moment in time, pain seared through her as her inner bear tore free. The Change was swift and fast, the sensation of pain thankfully leaving her just as quickly as it had come.

Jamie muttered in protest, dropped to his hands and knees and in a sizzling display of multicolored lights, made the Change beside her. His bear was so much bigger than hers, twice her size, his silky brown fur sprinkled with black along his ears and paws, his markings so different to her own. Her coat was a golden-white, almost an identical match to her pale hair.

He lumbered up to her, nudged her flank with his muzzle and pushed her toward the thick white mat at the end of the bed.

She allowed him to steer her there, to where the sunshine streamed in and warmed the spot so brilliantly. Down, she sat, then rolled onto her side and sheer happiness burst through her as he padded in behind her, settled on the floor and dropped one front paw over her rump.

With his claws, he lightly scratched her pelt.

Neither of them moved from that serene spot, his gentle petting soothing both her and her bear.

This was what she wanted, to lie with him and be so at peace. Only with him could she ever do so.

Another husky growl and his fur retracted, his muzzle shortening.

Jamie made the Change and she whimpered at the loss of his bear being gone.

"I'm still here," he murmured as he rolled her fully onto her back and caressed her exposed belly. How she wanted him to be rubbing her true flesh, just the two of them lying here skin-to-skin, only her bear was enjoying his touch too much to allow her to Change back.

"Your bear is so sweet and nothing like my ferocious beast." He bracketed his legs either side of her body and deepened his rub and when her purr got a hell of lot louder, he stroked down her front legs, caught her clawed paws and pressed them to his shoulders. "Change, now."

Molten heat rushed through her body at his commanding demand and she took back the control from her bear and forced the Change. All woman, she grasped his shoulders tighter and wriggled as he stretched out over top of her, his cock so big and rigid between them.

"This is sheer torture." He hissed out a breath. "My dick is about to snap in two."

"That sounds painful." She desperately wanted to slide her fingers between their bodies and take his cock in hand and alleviate some of that torture pulsing through him. She certainly wanted to caress his hot length and to learn how he liked to be touched.

"If you want me to back off at any time, then tell me and I will." His muscles and tendons flexed as he lifted up an inch, the challenge in his gaze clear to see. "Otherwise, put your hand on me."

"That's one challenge I intend to accept." She trailed one finger down his rock-hard chest then wrapped her fingers around his cock. Definitely big and rigid. "Tell me what to do to lessen your pain."

"Move your hand up and down." He dipped his head to her neck and kissed along the line of her throat.

She stroked him in long pulls and shuddered with delight, while he trailed his mouth down to her breast with delicious nips and soft kisses. Gently, he suctioned his mouth over one nipple and drew the bud in deep. He sucked, hard, and a tight kind of need unfurled between her legs, one she was certain only he could appease.

Rubbing against him, she tried to gain the friction she needed to ease her own fiercely rising ache and oh my—he pressed one knee between her inner thighs, right up against her lower folds and she whimpered as he gripped her hips and urged her to move on him. Move she did, the friction he offered exactly what she needed. It caused something so very heady and wanton within her to rise. "Give me your fingers," she whispered raggedly against his lips.

"Bella?" He slid his hand down her body, his fingers gliding over her slickness. "I want to make you come."

"I want to make you come as well."

"My bear is getting drunk on the scent and the taste of you. I'm losing control of both him and me. We need to stop, and we need to do it now before we go too far." He flicked one finger over her clit and she cried out as more pleasure assailed her. She climbed higher, toward a peak she only ever wanted to scale with him.

"Try to stop this moment from happening, and I'll bring out the claws."

"I can't take you in the way a mated male does with his woman, not when I've no idea if you're truly mine." He sucked in a deep breath. "And right now I'm so close to thrusting inside you. If I do, the wrath of our entire clan will fall down upon our heads."

Their clan. She had to consider their clan as well. Which she wasn't doing.

Damn it. One more blasted month and she'd know for certain if he was hers.

"Stop." She whispered the word then cried it out again as she pushed against his shoulders. A burning tore through her very soul as he rolled onto his back beside her and gulped in air. Chest rising and falling, she dragged in precious air too. "What do we do now?"

"This is all my fault. I'm the one who needs to do something." He pushed to his feet, hauled on his black boxers and standing at their connecting door with his back to her, muttered, "The SUV is yours. I'll leave the keys on my bed. I'm going lone bear until the next full moon rises. You know this needs to happen."

"You're leaving me, just like that?" She scrambled to her feet, nabbed his shirt and pulled it on. "Don't. We need to talk, not separate."

"I disagree." With a fierce scowl, he snapped at her, "Don't leave this room until I'm gone. You're not to follow me, not today, not tomorrow, not this month. I'll return to the keep before the next full moon, but don't expect that to be until the last possible moment." He left, shut the door behind him with a soft click, one which reverberated like thunder in her ears.

She should go after him, only she had to let him go as he'd requested.

Even she understood that this was the only way forward for them both.

Not that she cared for it, not one bit.

Chapter 6

At the bay, 1211.

"The inland caves I'm about to take you to, are very precious to my parents. The deepest cavern is the place where my father took my mother the night they first discovered their bond had taken form." Jamie stood near his half-beached skiff with Annabella on the curve of the cove where the soft sand remained dry. This woman had captured his attention years ago, and well before the last full moon had arisen and a bond had formed between them, one their fae kind desired with all their heart and soul, a bond they'd soon complete. Only a fortnight remained, and then they'd be able to speak vows. When they did, he'd make her his in every possible way.

"I hope 'twill be a most precious place for us too." The wind blew her glossy golden locks about, one strand fluttering free and swirling through the air.

"As do I." He plucked the strand out of the air before it could wisp away on the breeze, wound it around his finger then slipped it carefully inside the pocket of his black leather pants. "Are you ready? The caves are only a short walk away."

"I'm ready, and I would go anywhere with you." She

beamed and skipped around him. "Lead the way."

"Then come." With the skies darkening, he guided her toward the mouth of the river to one side of the cove then together, they trekked alongside the gurgling waters leading deeper into their clan land. The forest rose high either side of the stream, the dense pines thickening the farther they walked. Pine needles covered the trail and birds chirped from their nests in the canopy above, while higher still, two hawks soared as they caught the stronger air currents.

Onward, he tramped, one hand on Annabella's elbow to ensure she didn't lose her footing on the rough terrain. She bubbled with excitement, her cheeks flushed and eyes bright, then as they reached the craggy rocks rimming the underground inland cave, she gasped and clutched a hand to her mouth as she stared downward into the darkened basin below.

"I'll carry you." He scooped her up against his chest and she wound her arms around his neck, her fingers tangling in his hair.

"I'm so glad I convinced you to bring me here this day." She nuzzled his neck, the sensation of her exquisite touch so damn mesmerizing.

"In all truth, so am I." He'd hated keeping his distance from her of late, only his fear that he'd never be able to keep himself from touching her before they spoke vows had been the primary reason why he'd done so. Two more weeks, then he'd make her his.

Watching his step, he maneuvered down the edge of the rocky basin to the tunnel's entrance then set her gently on her feet and taking her hand, moved ahead of her to guide their way down the tight passageway of dirt and stone.

Water dripped from the gritty ceiling overhead and splashed his booted feet. As they trekked, the passageway darkened further and he kept one hand around her waist to ensure she didn't slip.

"Oh, we're almost there." Annabella squealed and rushed past him to the end of the tunnel. She tottered on the edge of the passageway and appeared ready to jump onto the soft sand surrounding the pool of hot water three feet below.

He caught up to her, his siren clothed in a gown of red wool with a tightly laced bodice trimmed in white lace. With her long golden locks swaying to her waist and her creamy skin all flushed, he could drown in the heavenly sight of her and be glad he had. Gently, he caught her hands, turned her to face him and pressed a kiss to each of her palms. "Wherever I lead, you'll follow."

"Aye, I shall always follow in your step." She pushed him back against the side of the tunnel, reached up on her toes and cupped his face in her hands. "I love you, Jamie."

"I love you too, Annabella, and I give you my word, from this day forth, I'll only ever lead us in the right direction."

He'd never break that promise, not even if his life depended upon it.

Chapter 7

Indulging himself in Bella wasn't permitted and should Jamie have allowed himself to continue petting her until she'd come, his actions would surely have come back to bite him in the butt. His bear wanted her, with a feral desire that would likely never be appeased, but he'd have to find a way to ensure it anyway. Only if she was truly his could he ever take things further with her, and for now, another twenty-nine more days must past before the next full moon rose and he knew for sure.

With his decision to go lone bear made, he'd dressed, shoved his belongings in his bag then leaving the keys as promised on his bed, trotted downstairs. He'd handed Gordon and Greer plenty of cash, more than enough to cover the damage he'd done to their wall then after a swift farewell, he'd trekked out on foot into the mountains.

The sexual attraction between him and Bella had been there since the first day she'd moved into her own chamber across the hallway from him, their joint desire for each other simmering right under the surface, but being paired together on this last mission had been a huge mistake.

If come the next full moon he discovered they weren't mated, then he might never recover from the agony that would surely take him.

* * * *

"Could I have been more stupid?" Annabella berated herself for millionth time as she stood at the window on the upper floor of the B&B, her gaze narrowed on the forest trail which Jamie had not long taken. He'd gone lone bear and that was all her fault. She'd pushed him too hard, virtually forced him into—

Ugh. Deep inside her heart, she'd wished to tempt his bear into mating with her when neither of them had truly known for certain if they were soul bound or not. Which meant with him disappearing and going lone bear, her kin were sure to question why. That meant there'd be hell to pay when she returned to the keep and she informed her fellow clansmen of what she'd done.

She rubbed her chilled arms, Jamie's last words reverberating through her mind.

Don't leave this room until I'm gone. You're not to follow me, not today, not tomorrow, not this month. I'll return to the keep before the next full moon, but don't expect that to be until the last possible moment.

At least she'd given him that, and allowed him to leave without following him.

She'd remained right where she now stood, her heart twisting all about as he'd strode across the clearing then disappeared into the forest without a backward glance. Now it was her turn to leave and since she had no intention of returning to Matheson Castle either, she too would go lone bear until the next full moon.

She'd make things right by both Jamie and the other unmated males by keeping to herself for a bit.

It was the only way.

She pulled on a pair of faded blue jeans, tucked the hem of Jamie's borrowed marbled gray shirt in, and buckled her boots. With wooden movements, she brushed her teeth and combed her hair before numbly scrawling a note to Hunter and slipping the folded paper into an envelope she'd found in the desk drawer.

Downstairs, she handed the letter to Greer along with the keys she'd collected from Jamie's bed and asked that she call Hunter later this afternoon and have him come and collect the vehicle. That should give her plenty of time to trek into the woods and ensure her ever diligent brother couldn't track her marks or follow her scent from here. Thankfully Greer hadn't questioned her request. This simply wasn't the time for her to seek comfort in her brother's hold, not when she'd put herself in this terrible predicament to start with.

Overwhelmed by guilt and her emotions teetering on the edge, she strapped her duffel to her back and took the opposite trail to Jamie. Hot tears streamed down her cheeks, her destination one which would take her far away from the one man she never wanted to leave, yet close enough to Matheson Castle so she wouldn't go completely insane over the month ahead. Empaths needed to be around others, but she'd now lost that right for the next twenty-nine days.

Aye, she'd head to the rustic cabin Murdock had built in secret for her and Isla almost four years ago. The chief had understood their needs back then even before they had, that they'd adore having somewhere to sneak away to for some much needed respite from time to time. She and Isla had indeed enjoyed their time away at the cabin, even kept a small supply of essentials there. The cabin would make the perfect place to hole up until the next full moon rose. So too Isla would know exactly where to find her. She sent a message through to her friend then powered her cell phone off.

Aye, this was the only way forward, for her, Jamie, and her entire clan.

* * * *

After tramping and not settling in any one place for several days, Jamie finally found the perfect spot deep within the forested ranges of the northern Highlands where few dared to tread. That suited him well since his bear was a ferocious beast to currently be around. He set up camp, hunted and fished and allowed his bear to take the lead as he roamed the land surrounding his campsite.

Exhausted at the end of each day, he slept like the dead, a welcome reprieve from his jumbled thoughts of Bella. She was the one woman he'd never wished to leave, yet also the one woman he might never be permitted near again.

That thought tore him up inside.

To never be able to look at her crushed his very soul into pieces, yet he had no one to blame but himself because of the liberties he'd taken with her. The mated bond was sacrosanct, and as yet one hadn't formed between them, which meant he'd gone too far in touching her.

The next full moon would decide his fate, a full moon he both longed for, yet also feared to the depths of his soul.

One in thirty-seven.

That was a chant he repeated over and over during the long days that passed as the month rolled on, and when the time finally came to make his way back down the mountains toward Matheson Castle, he'd finally gotten his thoughts and mind a little more in order.

Aye, he'd also lost a great deal of weight and now looked a whole lot meaner and leaner, but there was naught he could do about that. Running himself to exhaustion had allowed him to thankfully pull both him and his bear back into line, to hopefully prepare himself for what was to come.

In the dark, early hours before dawn, two days prior to the full moon's rising, he strode back through the postern gate, lifted a hand in greeting to the sentry posted on the ramparts above and without stopping to say hello or chat, bounded inside.

He took the stairs two at a time until he reached the top floor and not even looking at Bella's door, he opened his own across from hers. He threw his gear on his bed, marched into his bathroom and planted his hands on the silver-edged white vanity. His reflection in the mirror showed the feral gleam still burning bright in his eyes, not that he could do much about that. He'd gotten as close as he'd dared to that one all-important night before returning, and now he was here, he just needed to steer clear of Bella for a little bit longer.

Shaving off almost a month's worth of scruff wasn't easy. He clogged his shaver and had to finish the job with his dagger, but once he'd scraped his jaw clean, he hauled himself into the shower, turned the lever on and let the hot spray bounce off his shoulders and neck.

The pounding water worked its magic and after he'd scrubbed himself clean and made himself at least a little more presentable, he dried off and donned a billowy white shirt and belted his kilt at his waist. Wearing his clan colors reminded him of exactly where his loyalty must always lie, to his kin—all of his kin. Aye, he should find Murdock and report in, only he couldn't yet do that. First, he needed a training session to rid himself of the added frustration that returning had caused.

He strapped on his sword belt, his blade secured in the fine black leather sheath at his side then trod downstairs. In the great hall near the fireplace, Levi lay stretched out on one of the blue suede couches in tan pants and a forest-green shirt, his sword glinting in the firelight at his hip. He nudged Levi's arm until his cousin groaned and cranked one eye open.

"Is that you, Jamie?"

"Aye, it's me."

"You look like hell." With a crooked smile, Levi pushed to his feet and gripped his shoulder. "Lone bear, huh. How'd that go?"

"It isn't an experience I'd recommend, or at least not for nigh on a month."

"You've been sorely missed." Levi pulled him into a hug

and thumped his back. "It's about time you got back. Only two more days remain."

"Aye, two more days." His cousin was an unmated male just like him and a low snarl escaped him, his bear wanting those two days to be done. "I need a sparring partner."

"Sure, I'm up for a session in the yard, provided while we train you tell me exactly how you've been."

"I've survived the time, and I'm stronger because of it." He strode outside with Levi, directly to the center of the training yard then slid his sword free and swung. Levi blocked his fast move, their blades clashing dead center and steel ringing loud against steel.

Then they battled and Levi matched him blow for blow, their fierce fighting intense and exactly what he needed. "How is Bella?" he puffed out some twenty minutes later between swings.

"You haven't heard?" Confusion flickered in Levi's golden shifter eyes.

"My cell phone hasn't been charged in a month." Another savage swipe.

"Then I hate to be the one to tell you, but you aren't the only one who went lone bear twenty-seven days ago. So did Bella."

"What?" He stumbled, struggled to right himself again.

"It's true. Bella headed into the mountains the same day you did, and Hunter's been like a raging bear ever since. The chief apparently knows where she is, has assured us all that she's safe and well. She's due back tomorrow morning, although Hunter still wants her back here now."

"Where's Hunter? I need to talk—"

"I'm right here." Hunter strode out from under the eaves in jeans and a dark shirt, his sword already swinging in his hand and his fist clenched around the hilt. His golden shifter eyes glowed in the light flickering from the torches mounted on the stone walls, his look likely as feral as his own was after hearing Levi's staggering news. "I wouldn't mind a little sparring session with you myself. Out of the way, Levi."

"I had no idea she'd gone lone bear as I did." His mind fuzzed and a buzzing screeched in his ears. "I have to find her." The last thing he should be doing was fighting when he needed to make certain she was all right and he hadn't caused any lasting damage by leaving her as ruthlessly as he had.

"You're damn right she needs to be found, but that'll be by me. Not you, not when she clearly ran from you." Hunter struck and he met the sharp hit, the clang of their blades echoing all around. "She's an empath, Jamie. Going lone bear isn't good for her, and you left her at the MacDonald's B&B to return here, all on her own. That's when she got away, trekked into the woods and made certain I couldn't catch her scent. Even though the chief knows where she is and has assured me she's well, it's not good enough. It's been twenty-seven damn days and I—" Hunter's voice broke and he dropped his sword with a *clunk* and shoved him by the shoulders into the curtain wall at his back. "She's my sister. What the hell happened between you two that sent you both running in different directions? I trusted you to keep her safe."

"Since the chief knows where she is, I'll ask him to tell me. I'll find her and bring her home." No more waiting. He'd do whatever it took to track her down and bring her back to her kin. He wouldn't allow her to suffer such isolation another moment, not because of him.

"That wasn't what I asked." Hunter heaved his fist back, and Jamie held perfectly still for the blow. He deserved all the punishment coming to him, and Hunter knew it too going by the feral glint in his eyes. "Defend yourself, Jamie."

* * * *

On the front step of the log cabin overlooking the river weaving through the woods, Bella curled her hands around a mug of hot chocolate as the skies lightened and the dawn sun peeked along the horizon. The crisp scent of the pine trees permeated the air, the breeze rushing all around and swaying the thick boughs of the towering trees.

Footsteps clacked across the wooden floors of the main room and Isla stepped onto the front porch with her own hot chocolate in hand and eased down next to her. "I've plugged your cell phone into the charger so expect a few calls now that it's back online. Dad also sent me a message to pass along to you."

"What did the chief say?" She wasn't returning until tomorrow. She only needed one day to settle back in before her whole world would likely come crashing back down on her again. At least she'd had this past month to settle her thoughts and consign herself to what would soon be.

"Jamie's back and he and Hunter just came to blows in the yard, or I should say Jamie stood still while Hunter pummeled him."

"Is he hurt?" She was eager for any smidgeon of information on Jamie, even though she likely shouldn't be.

"There's a bruise or two, although Hunter stepped away when Jamie declared he had no intention of defending himself. Dad asked if you want to wait it out here until the full moon actually rises, and I think that might be best as well. We're only a mere half hour drive from the keep, an easy distance for your mate to track you down in two nights' time. There might be less issues if you actually stay here, but that's entirely up to you."

"You mean so Jamie can't halt my chosen one from his pursuit?" She'd confided in both Isla and their chief after she'd arrived here at the cabin, had actually found them both already waiting for her after Isla had received the text message she'd sent.

She'd told them everything, explained the vision and all, only their chief had simply clammed up on the issue of explaining anything to her. He'd simply said, "Not yet, Bella. I haven't *seen* the time is right."

Not very unhelpful.

"I agree the odds aren't in Jamie's favor, although there's always been something 'more' between you two." Isla stared at her hot brew then slowly sipped it.

"I can't help but feel hurt that he left me." Except his leaving had also been the only way, and even she'd understood that at the time.

"Let me show you the pics Dad sent through to me." Isla set her drink aside, opened her cell phone and flicked through her messages. When she got to the one she wanted, she turned the screen toward her.

An image of Jamie plastered to the curtain wall, half bent over with Hunter's fist in his belly, sent a spasm of pain shooting through her. Her bear whimpered deep inside her too, the sight of Jamie and her brother so at odds, paining her. "They're like brothers, and now I've likely destroyed that relationship by my actions. Jamie never wanted me to take things as far as I did. What happened between us was all my fault."

"You need to call Hunter and explain that then, and preferably before Jamie speaks to him and admits the truth." Her dearest friend arched a brow. "Jamie will do that soon. We're kin and never keep anything from each other for long."

"Jamie won't say a word if he believes that it'll bring any harm down upon my head."

"I agree. Jamie loves you, so he might withhold the information."

"He also deserted me."

"For a good reason."

"I know, but he still deserted me, and now I've deserted him, although all I can think about right now is how very right he was to leave me, and for me to leave him as well." She grasped her achy chest. "I'll go stir crazy if I wait here for another two days. One will be long enough. I want to return tomorrow morning. Will you come and collect me?"

"Of course. Do you want to speak to Jamie before the full moon?"

"Half of me does, and the other half doesn't." That conversation wasn't one she was looking forward to, not when she still wanted him so badly. "I don't want to hurt the other unmated males, or at least any more than I already have."

"I understand." Isla pocketed her cell phone in her jeans pocket and cupped her mug in both hands. A swirl of chocolate-scented steam drifted into the air. "I wanted my mate to be one of the unmated males within our keep, but instead Iain's from the other full-blooded shifter clan. I ran from him for five years since the last thing I ever wished to do was leave my father and my clansmen to join with him and his people. Thankfully though Iain allows me to stay here as often as I need to, which I had no idea he'd do at the time. Now I'd never look back, which means sometimes we need to experience heartache in order to discover the truth. You haven't let our clan down, and neither has Jamie. What you two did was simply kiss and take things a little too far. Maybe he's yours, maybe he isn't, but whatever happens I know you'll both work through any further problems that might arise."

"If he's not mine, I'm not sure I'll survive it. Wherever he leads, I've always—" *Followed*. That silent word rang with brutal strength through her mind.

"Then trust in your heart and what it's currently telling you, because those emotions are coming directly from within your very soul. Take some hope in that."

"My heart and soul are currently in turmoil." The ache in her chest throbbed deeper.

"Liam asked about you before I left the keep this morning as well." Quiet words, her friend's brow raised. "I told him your monthly flow arrived two weeks ago. I hope that was all right? He wanted to organize those blood tests on your return, but I told him not to bother."

"Thanks for telling him, and aye, I don't need those tests now." It had been as Jamie and Liam had said. She'd smelled ripe to them, and she certainly had been. "What else did Liam say?"

"That whatever imbalance caused your body to get mixed signals, must have corrected itself." She groaned and tapped her head. "It appears my time here is up. Iain is insisting I return."

Her friend had formed a merged link of the mind with her mate on the night they'd completed the bond, just as all mated shifter pairs did. A bond she longed for too, but only with Jamie. She stood, set her own mug of hot chocolate down and tugged the front zippered sides of her tan leather jacket together. "I'll walk you to your SUV."

"Thanks." Isla stood, rested her hand on the side post and rubbed the rise of her belly. She carried twin boys, both highly skilled seers, and their clan couldn't have been more excited when they'd heard the news. "Will you be all right for one more day? I can stay over tonight if you want."

"No, you go and snuggle up to your mate. I just needed the visit." She hugged her friend and not wanting to let her go, whispered, "Come back for me tomorrow morning, okay. I'm going to keep to my original schedule and return."

"You're squishing me again." Isla coughed. "That's one tight grip you've got."

"Stop complaining." She hugged her friend all the tighter. "I'll miss you."

"I'm right here, and only a phone call away now that your cell is charging."

"I'll still miss you." Empaths struggled to be away from their nearest and dearest, and she'd been no different this past month. "I miss everyone, Jamie included, and I hate how much I miss him."

More than hated it, yet still, each night when she'd fallen

into bed, she'd donned his marbled gray t-shirt and hugged his scent to her. It would be so easy to ring him right now since he'd returned and her cell phone was back on the charger, his too likely.

"See you tomorrow, bright and early." Isla kissed her cheek then walked down the front step and around to her vehicle parked on the rutted dirt track which led back to the main road.

She waved as her friend drove off.

All alone again.

She returned to the cabin with the mugs, picked up her cell phone and scrolled through the bombardment of messages, all of them dated from between the day she'd gone lone bear twenty-seven days ago until a mere five minutes past.

Liam had sent her a heart emoticon each and every day. Levi, Jamie's close cousin, had sent a plethora of happy faces with lipstick kisses all over them. She smiled, warmth infusing her. Hunter's messages scrolled by with "hurry up and ring me" over and over again, while not one message had come through from Jamie, not even since his return to the keep.

Tears sprang into her eyes.

Damn that man.

She wanted him with a desperation that bordered on insane.

* * * *

Jamie slumped on his bed after the fight of all fights with Hunter. He'd gone to see the chief afterward and speak to him, which had gotten him no closer to discovering Bella's whereabouts, other than learning she was still fine and well and would be returning early tomorrow morning. Twenty-four more blasted hours until he'd see her again and that wasn't good enough.

On his back, he gripped his cell phone attached to the charger, set the tracking app to go and jabbed in Bella's number. Hunter had said she hadn't yet returned any of his calls, as had Levi. She'd clearly turned her phone off, just as he'd done, but he had to start somewhere and it would be with placing a call to her.

A ringing buzzed in his ear. Not her automated answering message. A bonus. He tapped his leg as he waited. "Answer, Bella. Come on, please answer."

"Hello."

He fumbled with his phone as her sweet voice shimmered down the line. "Bella, where are you?"

A disconnect tone pulsed in his ear, and damn it, he wasn't having that. He punched in her number again, his bear riled and tearing for release inside him.

"I'm not talking to you right now, Jamie Matheson. Leave me alone," she growled as she answered on the first ring.

"Wait. Don't hang up. I need to talk to you. It's urgent."

"Is someone hurt? Because that's the only 'urgent' I'm listening to right now."

"You're hurting, and it's killing me. Allow me to apologize."

"You've got twenty seconds since I know you're as bad as Hunter and are likely tracing this call. Argh, I really shouldn't have let Isla turn my cell phone back on. Go."

Twenty friggin' seconds. He wanted to wrap his hands around her neck and throttle her, as well as kiss her silly. "I shouldn't have gone lone bear and deserted you."

"You left me for a very good reason. I pushed you too hard."

"You need to let me back in."

"I can't. I'm likely taking up with another man in two days and I'll be sleeping with him, for the rest of my life. I want his cubs, not yours. Never yours."

"You're trying to push me away on purpose. Stop it."

"You started it by leaving me, and now I'm finishing it."

"I want you, so bad, will always want you, no matter who you're mated to. That I promise you." A promise given, and a promise he would keep, for now and for all time.

"That I believe is our current problem." A beeping pulsed in his ear.

His twenty seconds were up.

He crunched the phone in his hand.

Chapter 8

Inside the cavern, 1211.

Standing at the edge of the tunnel, Jamie held Annabella in his arms. Her declaration that she loved him, would follow him wherever he led, made his heart lift with love and his chest pump out with proudness. Bringing her here to this sacred place where his parents had completed their bond had been right.

With one hand on the side of the entrance wall, he jumped off the three-foot ledge and landed with a clomp in the grainy white sand that rimmed the side of the cave. Then gently, he caught her around the waist and swung her down beside him where the water lapped onto the thin length of the beach. Steam plumed from the hot pool of water and swirled all around, its fresh scent sweet and warm, almost as sweet as Annabella's lily fragrance.

"This place is so peaceful and heavenly." She kicked off her slippers, dug her toes into the sand and let out a soft sigh. "'Tis no wonder your father brought your mother here the night they first discovered their bond had taken form." She stared up at the craggy ceiling where a vent allowed the moonlight through. The full moon's light dappled across the darkened surface of the pool and reflected against the slick rock walls in shimmery golden beams. "I would dearly love a swim."

"As would I." He removed his sword belt, propped it against a rock and divested himself of his wrist and ankle daggers then crouched at the water's edge and swirled a hand through the water. "This is the perfect heat."

"Wonderful." Annabella unlaced her red gown's front stays then pulled her arms out of the long clingy sleeves and pushed the woolen folds to the ground. In naught but her shift, which thankfully covered her to her ankles, she walked into the water and giggled. "This is beyond wonderful."

"Wait for me." He toed off his boots, loosened the ties of his black leather pants and pushed them down his legs then in his tunic fluttering at mid-thigh, strode into the water. "Stay close."

"I can swim without any issue, thank you." With a teasing grin, she walked backward and once she reached waist-depth, dove and disappeared below the surface.

He dove too, followed the flash of her white shift within the murky depths and as he caught up with her, snagged her around the waist and kicked them both upward. He broke the surface in a fizz of bubbles, the woman in his arms giggling with delight. "You're fast, my sweet Annabella."

"You're faster." Her lips now lifted in a sensual smile and she leaned closer, touched her forehead to his, and whispered, "You are my chosen one."

"Aye, as you are mine."

"There is naught I'd love more than to feel your hands on my bare flesh."

"I think not." He let her slide out of his arms, dunked under the water until it flowed over his head then kicked away. Once he'd made it to the far ledge rimming the pool, he hauled himself out of the water and sat on the edge.

His siren floated in the middle of the pool on her back, her hair spread like a lily pad of gold around her head, her nipples poking into the wet cloth of her white shift and a tease of her pink aureoles showing through. The sight stole his breath, although thankfully not his wits.

He'd never give into her, not when he had only another fourteen days to wait until she was in truth his wife. A slow smile lifted his own lips. This sacred place was all theirs, this moment in time one he'd forever cherish, and once the coming battle with their enemy was done, he'd bring her right back here after they'd spoken their vows and make sweet love to her. Only on that day would he ever give into his beloved siren.

"What has that smile on your face?" With one arched brow, she eyed him from the center of the pool as she scooped water at her sides.

"I'm planning our wedding night." He stroked her body with his gaze, from her lush lips to her tiny toes. "And our first kiss."

"So, I truly must wait another fortnight? I have no' tempted you into anticipating our wedding night this very day?"

"Aye, you are a terrible temptation, but we shall both wait. I willnae bring any dishonor down upon your head."

"I love you, Jamie." That love shone bright in her eyes as she straightened and treaded the water in one place.

"I love you too, Annabella. You're mine, always mine."

A promise given, and a promise he would keep, for now and for all time.

Chapter 9

No matter who Bella was mated to, Jamie would always want her and a promise given, was a promise he'd always kept. Find her this day, he would and once he had, he'd ensure she knew just how very much he already loved her.

Aye, he loved her, and he had to believe that the two of them were soul bound, that she belonged to no other. She was his very heart and soul, and no matter they still had two more days to go until the full moon rose, he wanted her back in his arms.

She'd also said she shouldn't have let Isla turn her cell phone back on, which meant the two of them had been together only a short time ago. He'd find Isla, see if he couldn't persuade her to give him Bella's location, because waiting another twenty-four hours for her return would surely turn him into a crazy beast of a man.

He tore through the keep searching for Isla and finally found her alone in the briefing room at the window. She stood watching the midmorning sun glimmering over the blue-green waters of the loch, the treetops rising high in the distance. He closed the door and marched across to her. "We need to talk."

"We do?" Brow wrinkled, she faced him, her long legs encased in jeans and her dark hair sweeping down her back in glossy waves. Concern radiated out from her golden shifter eyes. "If this is about Bella, then she knows you and Hunter came to blows in the yard."

"I just spoke to her on the phone and now I need to know exactly where she is."

"I can't tell you, not any more than I could tell Hunter."

"Could you at least give me a hint?" He'd fall at her feet and beg if he needed to.

"No."

"I've hurt her and it's tearing me up inside. I need to apologize for what I've said and done." He slid his dagger free of its sheath and held it out toward her hilt first. "The only way I'll remain here, is if you stab me and ensure I can't get back up again. I will find her, although I'd rather have a little help from you first. The sooner I get to her, the better."

"I could pass on a message and your apology, but that's all I'm willing to do. No directions to where she's staying."

"A message then. Call her now and I'll wait while you get her on the phone." He lowered to one knee. "Please, Isla. Take pity on me. I'm a broken man at the moment, one desperate to make amends."

"Oh boy, I can't believe you're actually begging." Smiling, she ruffled his hair. "Get up and I'll make the call. You tell me what you want to say and I'll repeat it." Isla punched in the number, set it to speaker and the blessed sound of the ringing tone soothed a touch of his frayed nerves as he rose to his feet.

"Hey, Isla." The sweet sound of Bella's voice as she sing-songed Isla's name soaked into him.

"Jamie's with me. He wants to apologize and I'm going to pass that along, plus a message from him. You ready?"

"Bella," he said and snuck Isla's phone from her hand and took it off speaker. With it pressed to his ear, he ducked around the large table while Isla frowned at him but thankfully didn't bother with a chase. With one eye on Isla, he paced before the big screen on the wall and continued, "I never wanted to tell you this across such a distance, but you've left me with no choice. You're one frustrating woman."

"You call that an apology?"

"I'm sorry, and I'm also coming."

"Coming where?"

"For you."

"Got any ideas where you should be heading to, my bossy bear?" Birds chirped and a splashing echoed back at him. She was outside, near a waterway of some sort. Aye, Bella might have put herself into isolation by going lone bear, but she'd never be able to do so without remaining at least a little close to her loved ones. She'd certainly never be able to head right across country, or at least he damn well hoped she wouldn't have.

"Not one, but full moon or not, I'm not leaving you alone another night."

"I'm returning in the morning."

"I can't wait another day to see you again, and a word of warning. When I find you, I'm going to pick up from where we left off, and I don't mean from this conversation, but from when we last shifted together. My bear is going to get drunk on the scent and taste of you, and I'm going to let him."

"P-pardon? N-no, you can't."

"I can, and if you try to stop me, I'll bring out the claws."

"We might not be mated."

"The one thing I've recognized since my return home, is that my heart tells me we are. I wouldn't be this crazy in love with you otherwise." He lowered his voice. "I'm a mess without you."

"It's not about what the heart wants, only the soul."

"My soul has been yours for a very long time." No other words had ever felt so very right coming from his lips. "Don't you remember? Wherever I lead, you'll follow? You told me I was your chosen one, just as I told you that you were mine. We were in the underground cavern, swimming in the pool where my parents—wait." He scrubbed a hand furiously across his brow. That hadn't happened, ever.

"Jamie, are you all right? What pool are you talking about?"

Images flickered in his mind and he closed his eyes and grasped ahold of them.

His sweet little Annabella floated on her back in the middle of the pool within the darkened depths of a cavern, her hair spread like a lily pad of gold around her head, her nipples poking into the wet cloth of her white shift and a tease of her pink aureoles showing through. The sight stole his breath. She was his beloved siren.

"*What has that smile on your face?*" With one arched brow, she eyed him from the center of the pool, no not him, she eyed a man seated on the ledge along from him, a man who looked like him in every way, the same man and woman from his first vision of them back at the B&B almost a month ago.

"*I'm planning our wedding night,*" the man answered as he gazed at the woman. "*And our first kiss.*"

"*So, I truly must wait another fortnight? I have no' tempted you into anticipating our wedding night this very day?*"

"*Aye, you are a terrible temptation, but we shall both wait. I willnae bring any dishonor down upon your head.*"

"*I love you, Jamie.*" That love shone bright in her eyes.

"*I love you too, Annabella. You're mine, always mine.*"

"Jamie?" Bella's voice rolled over him and he shook his head, dragged himself back to the present. "What was that I just saw? I had another vision." Her voice was all wobbly.

"So did I. Annabella and Jamie were swimming within an underground pool, deep within the earth. Did you catch the same vision as me again?"

"I did, but I'm not sure what it all means."

"Neither am I, except for the fact that I want the mated bond with you, and I won't allow anyone else to steal it from me.

We almost had it once—I mean—I think there was a battle, a bad one. We never completed the bond and we should have. It's my fault we've spent centuries apart." He had no idea what was with this tumble of words coming from his mouth, only that they felt incredibly right.

"What did you just say?" A woodpecker rapped away, or perhaps that was her tapping her foot. The whirring of an engine resounded, there one moment and gone the next. Likely that of a water pump starting and stopping, or something very similar.

"Give me your coordinates."

"No, I need to think this all through. I'll see you tomorrow, when I return. We'll wait until the full moon rises and see what happens."

"It'll be too late by then." In the past it had been, and he wouldn't let that happen again. Damn these crazy stirrings in his mind. "Do you want me as greatly as I want you?"

No answer, then the phone beeped and the connection was gone.

His bear roared forth and head lifted, he howled.

* * * *

Of course she wanted him.

Lugging in a breath, Bella turned off the hose beside the porch where she'd been watering the garden when Isla had called. It was just as well she wasn't anywhere near Jamie right now, because she'd certainly give into him within a heartbeat, and what was with that second vision? Two now, and both so damn confusing.

Overhead a bird soared and a woodpecker drilled its beak into the trunk of a tall pine. She gathered in the hosepipe and set it the corner near the porch. Jamie would never be able to find her out here, not when Hunter hadn't, and her brother was one of the best trackers in their clan. Of course so was Jamie, but still, she should be safe until tomorrow.

She ducked back inside the cabin and wandered through the

lounge to the bedroom with its compact bunked beds for two, stripped off her jeans and t-shirt now the sun had risen higher and changed into a short white skirt and the matching white cropped top with a lacy hem that left two inches of her midriff bare. With her hair lying loose and long, she packed a small backpack with a few essentials, sunscreen and sunglasses, a light jacket in case it cooled down later, and a couple of honey sandwiches and an apple and water bottle. She toed on a pair of flats she'd left beside the front door, locked the cabin and stowed the key under the earthenware pot holding a lush fern on the top step.

The inland cavern where she'd swum each day wasn't far from this spot, a half-hour walk and no more, a cavern appearing very similar to that which she'd just seen in her vision. She'd go there again today, swim and consider all that had just happened.

With a floppy hat on her head, she trekked alongside the gurgling waters of the river, the sun rising higher and streaming through the leafy golden-green foliage overhead. Along the pine-needle covered trail, she strolled, the birds cheerily chirping in their nests above and the odd hawk soaring within the circular air currents. She loved exploring the wilds of Scotland, but for the past month she'd taken great care to keep her scent to this trail alone since her kinsmen rarely trod this area.

Onward, she tramped until she reached the craggy rocks rimming the caves then she stowed her flats in her bag and barefoot, maneuvered down over the rough stones into the basin of the cave entrance below. When she made the tunnel leading ever deeper into the depths of the earth, she pulled out her flashlight and shone the beam over the musty dirt and stone encrusted walls.

Water dripped from the rocky ceiling overhead and splashed into puddles at her feet. She continued on, mud oozing between her toes and her bear fairly purring with pleasure. Being amongst nature, in its most pure and isolated form as she was today, always excited both her and her other half.

As she reached the end of the tunnel, she flicked off the torch and jumped off the three-foot high ledge and landed with a soft thump on the white sand below. Here, light trickled in through a natural vent overhead and she dug her toes into the warm grains and dropped her bag beside a slick rock just out of reach of the water lapping onto the small curve of the beach. Steam rose from the hot pool and permeated the air with its heavenly fresh scent. Perfect. This place called to both her and her bear, and aye, this cavern was the one from her recent vision. She couldn't mistake that now.

Slowly, she shimmied her skirt to the ground, dropped her top onto the pile too and in her flesh-colored panties and bra, walked into the water and once she reached waist-depth, dove and immersed herself completely in the warmth of the pool.

Peace overflowed her.

This was exactly where she needed to be.

* * * *

In the rear parking lot, his satchel holding supplies tossed into the back seat of his black SUV, Jamie spread the aerial map of the forested land surrounding Matheson Castle out on the hood and tapped the crinkled paper with one finger. Rivers and waterways ran plentifully through their land, but not any dwellings that required a water pump.

Hmm, Bella couldn't be too close, otherwise their patrolling men would've picked up her scent, which left the far perimeter of their land as the most viable option where they patrolled the least, or of course even farther afield. In all truth, she could be anywhere, but his gut told him she had to be somewhere on their Matheson land since she'd never be able to go lone bear too far from her kin, not to mention Isla had visited her just that morning. She had to be within an hour's drive.

He slid behind the wheel and drove out of the lot and along the gravel road. With his window cranked down, he breathed deep of the fresh Highland air and turned it over as he searched it for even a trace of his sweet little bear.

With his gut leading him, he bumped across the rough terrain, the sun high overhead. Fifteen minutes later, he passed a washed-out side road with fresh tire tracks embedded in the two dirt channels where weedy grass grew knee-high in the center strip and along either side. That side road led to the river and nowhere else, so likely a fisherman had recently driven down there, although as he continued on, his chest squeezed in on itself and he braked, checked his rearview mirror and reversed.

Some of his tension eased, as if his very soul were beckoning him to take that trail.

He jerked the wheel and bumped down the side road.

Two miles in, he came to the end of the track and parked on the thick grass next to the boulders where the river water washed downstream in a fast flow. Nose to the air, he sniffed. Nope, there was nothing out here but the fresh earthy scents of the forest and a great fishing spot.

Back behind the wheel, he did a U-turn then halted at the sight of a break in the dense tree line where another track meandered off. One a vehicle would have trouble negotiating since the brush and brambles grew so thick. Their clansmen never patrolled beyond this point, not when Murdock did so as needed. Their chief's late wife had adored this area and he and his clansmen considered the land beyond this spot by the river sacred. Only Murdock and Isla ever—wait. Isla visited this area and knew it well.

He swung down the trail. It was tight, the brush scraping the sides of his vehicle and pinging the undercarriage. Another fifteen minutes on and he weaved out of the woods and into a small clearing with a quaint log cabin and a stream meandering nearby.

Well, this was a surprise. The chief must've built this cabin here without telling any of them. Certainly he'd never mentioned it before.

He hopped out, slammed the door and rested his butt on the hood.

All around, the forest rose toweringly tall, birds chirping and more than one woodpecker tapping away within the high trunks of the surrounding pines. Clothes flapped from a hemp rope strung between two trees and he pushed off the hood and jogged across to the line, unpegged a red bra and brought the silky fabric to his nose. The aroma of sweet lilies had his bear rolling around inside him.

Fuzzy-headed, he unpegged more clothes, a red and white striped skirt and red tank top, two pairs of shorts and a lightweight zippered jacket, panties as well. Bella's scent washed over him, her exotic fragrance affecting him far stronger than ever before.

A little drunk on her scent, he stuffed the bra and panties in his sporran, loped back to the SUV and with his backpack in hand, folded the rest of her clothes inside. Claws slicing in and out, his bear roared for his mate. *Find her*, his beast demanded. *Make her ours.*

He checked both doors and every window of the cabin. All locked up, although it was a small abode with a basic kitchen and seating area, a bedroom with two bunks and a bathroom outfitted with the bare necessities, a shower cubicle, toilet and vanity by the looks as he wandered around and checked each window. No sign of Bella inside. He worked the clearing in a crisscross pattern and picked up more of her delectable scent in the grass. Just enough to guide him toward where she'd gone.

Backpack strapped on, he trekked away from the cabin.

Following the gurgling stream, he weaved his way along the cusp of their Matheson land toward the—hold on. His vision this morning had shown him a cavern with a hot pool, an inland cavern on Matheson land. There were a number of them scattered about, but only one of those sacred places drew him toward it now.

He'd been a lad of twelve the last time he'd tramped out here. Hunter, Levi and Liam had been with him at the time. The four of them had decided to go on an overnight hunt and they'd ended up at the inland cavern with its entrance deep within a basin of rocks. They'd explored the darkened passageways within the caves, even swum and stayed overnight on a patch of grainy sand next to a hot pool. He'd had a blast and when he'd left the next day, it had been with a heavy heart. He hadn't wanted to leave, not one bit. Something about the place had soothed his very soul.

It could be the cavern from his vision, but he couldn't be certain unless he checked it out. So many underground caves could be found on their land.

As the sun began its descent, the dappled light filtering through the foliage overhead dimming, birds chirped and the odd hawk soared within the strong air currents high overhead. Bella's tracks in the mossy bank kept him on the right path and when he reached the edge of the rocky basin to the cavern, he maneuvered down over the rough stones and into the entrance below.

Flashlight in hand, he shone the beam over the dirt and stone encrusted walls as he negotiated the passageway. It was far tighter than he last remembered, although mayhap that was because he was bigger.

Water dripped from the musty ceiling overhead and splashed his feet, the ground mucky underfoot and Bella's footprints nice and fresh and easy to follow. His bear grizzled under his skin, demanding he hurry his pace and once he reached the end of the tunnel, he stood at the edge of the three-foot ledge and jumped.

White sand crunched under his booted feet and a woman splashed in the darkened depths of the pool just beyond the beach, steam swirling all around as she moved onto her back and floated. Like his vision from earlier this morning, his Bella appeared the same as the Annabella from ancient times with her golden locks spread around her face.

In naught but a nude bra and panty set, her sleekly muscled body on full display, his seductive siren swam as if she had not a care in the world. His bear snapped and snarled within him, suddenly wanting out and he lifted his head and roared.

* * * *

A bellowing roar ricocheted against the rock walls and Bella gasped and went under. She came back up spluttering, shoved her wet hair out of her face and froze in shock at the sight of Jamie standing on the sand. He glared at her with pure frustration, anger, and intense desire flaring in his golden shifter eyes, those same emotions rushing out and swamping her. Oh boy, it appeared she'd made him mad, in every possible way.

"How on earth did you find me?" He never should have been able to and before she sank under the surface again, she kicked and treaded water to keep herself afloat.

"I allowed my instincts to guide me." He removed his sword belt, propped it against the rock next to her belongings, divested himself of his sheathed daggers and dropped his backpack on the ground. Boots unlaced, he straightened to his full height, unbelted his sporran and kilt. His tartan slithered to his feet, the hem of his white tunic thankfully still covering him adequately, although with his gaze on her, the promise in his eyes was clear to see. He intended to join her without a stitch of clothing on.

"We are not reacquainting ourselves with each other right now, not when the full moon has yet to rise. We've one more full day."

"You're the only one both me and my bear want. We've hunted you down, and now we intend to capture and contain you."

"Contain me how?"

"With my body." He whipped his tunic over his head and

his cock, so full and thick, bobbed against his belly, the head flaring a rich plum color and his balls tightening and drawing upward as his shaft rose ever higher. Across the banded width of his abs, bruises darkened his flesh and he growled low in his throat and flexed his chest muscles.

"Hunter shouldn't have laid a hand on you."

"With my shifter blood, I'll heal quick enough. May I join you?"

"You're actually asking?" Something deep within her stirred at the delicious sight of him. His body was all steadfast power and roped tendons. As he planted his feet wide, her breasts swelled with needy demand and her nipples pinched tight. This moment was inevitable. This morning on the phone he'd said that he wanted the mated bond with her, that he wouldn't allow anyone else to steal it from him. That they'd almost had it once. Something about a battle, a bad one, and that they'd never completed the bond and should have. It was his fault they'd spent centuries apart. She shook her head. For some reason, in this most sacred of places, his strange words had never made more sense. Hands shoved behind her, she flicked the clips free on the back of her bra, removed it then hooked her panties off her legs under the water. She balled both scraps of silk in one hand and tossed them to him. "There's your answer. I can no more deny this moment than you can."

He caught her lingerie mid-air, dropped them on top of his clothes then burst forward. Into the water, he plowed, dove and disappeared under the surface. Waves rippled toward her then his murky shadow appeared for a mere moment before he emerged in a spray of water with a hungry grin lifting his lips. "I've missed you."

"I've missed you too." She wrapped her arms around his neck and he took her weight easily as he treaded water for them both. "This morning on the phone, my vision was about Annabella and Jamie, both right here in this pool. She was floating on her back while he sat on the ledge behind her. He wanted to wait until their wedding night before he completed the bond, and she didn't. She loved him, didn't care to wait, although he loved her too and had no intention of bringing any disgrace down upon her head by anticipating their vows. It was as if I was in her head and yet not. I certainly caught his deep love and devotion for her through my empath skill."

"I've no idea what these two visions we've both seen are about, but this couple looks just like us and even holds our names."

"We need to speak to Murdock and tell him exactly what we've both seen—see if he can bring some light to it all. He hasn't been helpful so far, but maybe if we both demand an answer, he'll give it to us." She touched his cheek where another bruise marred his flesh there. "You should shift now. I don't like seeing these bruises on you."

"I'll shift when you shift." His husky words sent a shiver of need pulsing through her.

"I can't fight this attraction I have for you, not even if I wanted to." She settled one hand on his chest, the heavy beat of his heart beyond soothing and everything within her settled further. The anxiety which had consumed her this past month fully eased and with a soft sigh, she swept her hand down his body and under the water, curled her fingers around his heavy shaft. Looking deep into his eyes, she gave him her promise. "Wherever you lead, I shall follow."

"I give you my word, from this day forth, that I'll only ever lead us in the right direction."

"Which direction would that currently be?" She grinned, hopeful of his answer being what she desired too.

"The full moon rises tomorrow night, and even though I want to complete the bond now, in order to respect the laws of our clan I'll wait. For now though, I intend on loving you however I possibly can."

"I can work with that." She leaned in and nipped his lower lip. "Will you truly finish what we began at the B&B?"

"Aye, I intend on giving you my claiming mark and to make you come." The water's surface rippled as he kicked her backward toward the ledge rimming the rear of the pool and hands on her waist, he lifted her onto the edge and heaved himself up beside her. He tipped her onto her back, his gaze moving down her body, his eyes gleaming a molten gold in the touch of light filtering through the vent high above. Streaks of sunset red washed through the darkening blue, the end of the day so close.

"Jamie, I long for the merged link of the mind, to be able to speak with you at will." When mated pairs of shifter blood fully joined together as one, a telepathic connection formed between them. She wanted that connection, and she intended on forging it with him as soon as their mated bond took form. One more day. She had to keep the faith that they were destined to be together. Grasping his broad shoulders, all wet and gleaming under the steam swirling all around them, she murmured, "I believe I've loved you for a very long time. If that makes sense."

"From this day forth, my heart will only ever beat for you." He caught both of her hands, gently uncurled her fingers and spread her palms against his chest, right over the pounding beat of his heart.

"Kiss me. Please, kiss me." She couldn't keep those whispered words at bay.

"And where should I start with those kisses?" A hungry rumble resounded in his throat as his gaze slid to her breasts. He cupped both mounds in his hands, weighed them together then bent his head and with one dark lock curling across his forehead, licked one nipple.

"That spot works for me." The velvety hot stroke of his tongue across the tip sent a bolt of liquid heat surging straight to her core and she arched into him, sank her hands deep into his hair and clung to him. "Do that again."

"Aye, I intend to." He swirled around the other tip, sucked her nipple deep into his mouth and sent a torrent of tingles racing through her. So sweetly, he treasured her, his greedy hunger making her moan for even more. She ached to join their bodies together fully as one, would struggle not to push for more this night as they touched each other so freely, but she needed to respect the other unmated males. For her clan's sake.

For now though, he was all hers. She reached down between them, stroked over the ridged bands of muscle across his stomach, his abs honed to contoured perfection from both his time going lone bear and the sheer hours of sword training he undertook each day. Carefully, she slid her fingers through the thatch of dark curls covering the apex of his groin then grasped the heat of his shaft and fondled the head. She caressed his hot flesh, from tip to the root, over and over again until he groaned something wicked.

"Bella, no more touching me right now. I'm on the edge of my control as it is." He edged back and she lost her hold on him, although he went no further. Breathing deep, he waited there, then when he seemed to gather his control, he skimmed his warm hands down her sides and along her outer thighs, heat racing along the entire path he touched.

Gently, he scooped her bottom, caressed her lower cheeks then puffed hotly against her belly as he nibbled across the flat plane of her stomach.

Her body lifted into his touch and her very soul soared higher, while overhead through the vent, the sunset red disappeared within the inky blue and the heavy golden weight of an almost full moon shimmered with a stunning display of stars twinkling all around it. This night would be theirs, each freely giving themselves to the other, this memory one she'd forever cherish.

Surrounding her, so hot and hard, he glided his fingers

along the inside of her thigh and craving an even deeper touch, she eased her legs farther apart, her mind racing in so many different directions. Never could she have accepted another man's touch this easily, not if he weren't to be her chosen one. Aye, tomorrow night he'd be the one who joined her in the courtyard as the full moon rose, and of that she no longer had any doubt.

He would be the one to sweep her up and carry her back to his bed.

He would be the one to make love to her throughout the night.

And he would be the one to bind them together in the way that mated pairs did.

"Do you trust me?" he whispered as he swept his hand over her entrance, his intimate touch scalding her deep within.

"With my very heart and soul, my bossy bear."

"Then relax and enjoy." He plunged one finger inside her, stroked deep and made her cry out as he curled into a spot that had her panting for more.

Enjoy, she would.

Eyes closed, she held on for dear life as he bent his head and licked along her inner thigh, his breath pulsing hotly against her skin as he rubbed her clit with his thumb. "Please, Jamie, please." She speared her fingers into his hair and caressed his scalp. "More."

"As you wish."

He spread her legs even wider and licked her flesh in the most intimate way. Moaning, he flicked his tongue over her clit and such exquisite pleasure roared through her. He was about to make her come, and she wanted to fall into pieces only in his arms.

"Don't hold back. Seek your pleasure, my sweet little bear." He sucked and her core pulsed and shattered as wave after wave of pure bliss rocked through her. She lifted free of her body and soared as a bright burst of colors ricocheted all about behind her closed eyelids.

"I want to be inside you so bad." He crawled up her body and captured her mouth in a hot kiss as he continued to stroke one finger deep inside her below.

Such a world of new sensation held her within its thrall, yet still she wanted more, to experience whatever he could give her in whatever time they had together tonight. She wrapped her hand around his length and instinct took over. Stroking him in long pulls, she increased her rhythm until he clenched his butt and rocked overtop of her.

"Hell, that feels incredible. Go faster, harder." He inserted a second finger into her and increased his own rhythm, his thumb rubbing over her sensitive clit with each swipe in and out and making her climb back to the very edge of the cliff she'd not long soared from.

"Oh, sooo good." She rocked with him as her second orgasm built.

"This is far more than good. It's incredible." He broke their kiss and laved the skin of her neck. He sucked her flesh between his lips and the thought of his bite sent a renewed wash of heat roaring through her.

Cupping the back of his head, she held his mouth firm against her neck and scraped her own teeth back and forth along his neck. No hesitation.

"I want your claiming mark now, Bella. From this day forth, we shall always bear each other's marks."

"I want that too." His enticing words had her rocking underneath him and no longer could she halt her body's need to move as one with him. She licked his racing pulse point.

"On the count of three, my love." He wedged his cock firm against her hip and sucked on her neck. "One—"

She wrapped her legs around the backs of his legs.

"—two," he rasped.

She clamped down on his neck, sank her teeth fiercely into him, and he lifted his head and roared.

"Three," he bellowed and bit her hard and fast in return, his mouth and teeth so wickedly firm against her flesh.

She cried out at the intense joining of their claiming marks, his bite sending her channel into contracting spasms. So exquisite. She flew to the stars, her inner muscles squeezing and dragging at his fingers within her.

"Got to come, too." With a pained expression, he pulled his fingers from her, grasped his cock and kneeling between her legs, looked deep into her eyes. "Breasts, belly, or below?" he grunted. "I need to mark you with my scent as well."

"Below."

"Good choice." One quick thrust and he came, his seed spurting from him in an arc and coating her mound.

His seed dribbled down the inside of her leg and she wriggled up onto her knees, wrapped her arms around his neck where he knelt and claws slicing free, dug them into his back. She didn't break his skin, but she had to have gotten damn close. With her mouth on the other side of his neck, she bit down a second time and marked him good and proper, just as any woman would do with her mate.

He was her chosen one, and tomorrow night, she intended for him to be her lover for life as well.

Naught else would she ever accept.

Chapter 10

A whirlpool of such need still swirled through Jamie even though he'd just come. So too did a powerful hit of fear. Losing Bella now he'd touched her so intimately, would kill him. She had to be his. He and his bear would never survive it if another of his clansmen sensed the mated bond forming with her and took her for himself. Hell, he didn't doubt he'd fight that man to the death in order to claim her instead.

With desperation and passion still slamming through him, he tipped her head gently to the side and eyed her throbbing pulse point. Mouth lowered to her flesh, her heartbeat skittered out of time under his lips and as he sank his teeth into her a second time, he marked her good and proper.

His beast roared, clawing for release while the man wanted only to thrust balls-deep inside her. He wanted to bury his cock so fully within her channel, to have his essence pulsing from him and coating her womb. He wanted to be the man who lived a lifetime with her, who gave her his undivided love and a huge litter of cubs, and he damn well wanted to start on all of that now.

He breathed deep, scented the air and released a low growl

that rumbled from deep within his chest. She smelt so completely intoxicating, far more than usual, like sweet honey mixed with fragrant lilies and another heady aroma that stated—hell, their shifter males could scent when their women were at their most fertile, as well as the change within them when they conceived, and his woman's scent called to the very heart of both him and his bear. She was beyond ripe.

Gently, he laid her back down on the ledge and she stretched underneath him as he wrapped himself around her, her lush breasts poking into his chest and tempting him beyond his endurance. The beaded tips, so pink and pointy snagged his attention and he laved the sweet treat, her long slender neck now bearing his mark in two places. Downward, he trailed, smattering her flat belly in kisses. "I want to mate. To give you a cub. You need to push me away for a bit, otherwise I might give into that want." He looked into her eyes. "Please, Bella, do this for me."

"Of course." She pushed against his shoulders and wriggled out of his hold, then she swept her legs over the side of the ledge and suddenly dropped down into the water. When she came back up, she planted her hands on the ledge and lifted back onto it. On her bottom beside him, she scooped another handful of water and splashed his cock clean. "Ridding us both of each other's scent will help ease your struggle. Is that better?"

"I'm not sure. Right now all I want to do is cover you in my scent all over again." He leaned in closer, licked along the upper swells of her breasts and she purred, caught his face between her hands and smiled so damn seductively that his cock filled and lengthened again, as if he hadn't just come.

"Do I need to give you my back?" Grinning, she shuffled around, looped her hair out of the way over one shoulder and tipped her head to the side.

The alpha bear in him rumbled his approval at her clear sign of giving him such authority over her, and he ran one finger along her neck and down her back. The ledge was hard and a little rough in places, and two scrapes marred her flesh, one on each rounded cheek. He shouldn't have taken her right here on this slab of rock, should have considered her wellbeing and instead chosen a softer bed, like the sand where the water lapped in. "I want you to shift so these marks heal. Bring your bear forth."

"Those are mere scratches. Ignore them."

"Your bear loves the water. Let's play for a bit." He scooped her up into his arms and dangled her over the water. "Shift."

"She'd rather come forth after she's been satisfied by you once more." She hooked her arms around his neck and clung. "I'm so hungry for more of your touch. I can shift later."

"You'll do as you're told and shift now."

"I clearly shouldn't have given you my back. It's made you twice as territorial over me." Smiling so enticingly, she rubbed her breasts against his chest. "That also makes me really hot."

"Shift."

"Mmm, very hot." More rubbing, her hand sliding down between them and encircling his stiff shaft. Such a buzz of sensations stormed his body, his head clouding over and his thoughts scattering.

Groaning, he lowered her feet onto the ledge and with a swish of his hands, he lifted her with his telekinesis and sent her floating out over the water and away from him, her toes skimming the surface. "Now, shift."

"Not fair." Pouting, she struggled mid-air, her arms waving about and her beautiful breasts bobbing all over the place. "Put me down, Jamie Matheson. I want to keep touching you."

"You can once you make the Change." He jumped into the water, the depth just along the ledge chest height on him, then with his skill he gently guided her down, just an inch or two, until her feet were submerged in the water. With the softest touch, he trailed his fingers along the gentle curve of her calves.

"I want more making-out time." She growled under her breath, her arms still flailing as she tried to snatch ahold of him but managed to get no closer. "You're annoying sometimes."

"That's just your feisty bear talking. She's on the cusp of full maturity and heckling for satisfaction." With another swish of his fingers, he turned her around until her very tight ass floated at a kissable distance, the scrapes along both cheeks calling out for his touch. He smacked his lips against first one rounded cheek then the other, gave each mark a lick and muttered, "Now bring out your little bear."

"Lower me some more and I might."

He could concede to that. With a mere thought from his mind alone, he galvanized his skill and turning her, drew her down farther, until most of her legs were submerged and her breasts bouncing at his head height. Gently, he blew on each beaded tip until her nipples puckered even tighter. Aye, he needed another taste of those sweet treasures. With his bear humming his pleasure, he scraped his teeth over both beaded points, razzed them and played his tongue over the tips.

"Oooh, now that's what my bear wants. Give her more of that." She sank her hands into his hair and kept his mouth positioned right where she wanted him. "Clever bear," she murmured.

"Hungry bear." He kissed around each mound, nipped her skin and left a dotted line of bites as she dug her fingers even firmer into his scalp.

"Sexy bear." A throaty purr rumbled in her chest and vibrated against his lips as he sucked on her breasts.

"She wants you to stake your claim on us."

Hell, his bear was losing all focus. She was supposed to be shifting, only the honey-rich scent now pooling again between her thighs had him losing his focus. He shook his head, tried to find a smidgeon of rational thought, only his bear overrode it all.

"Jamie?" She stroked his nape, the back of his neck so

sensitive to her exquisite touch.

"Keep touching me, Bella." Another demand as he lowered her further and bent his head over the tempting curve of her neck. "I need to bite you again."

"Aye, please." She made a hot, needy sound low in her throat and he pressed an open-mouthed kiss against the hollow of her throat before sucking her skin deep inside his mouth. "Make sure you mark me well. I'm all yours, will never belong to any other."

So serious, and her demand both calmed his bear and made him rise to dominance. Damn right, she was all his. Never would she belong to any other, other than him.

He slid one hand down her body, covered her belly with his palm and with a piercing need he couldn't hold back, bit down hard on her neck where her shoulder curved into it, this time drawing a trickle of blood.

She heaved against him, her entire body shuddering with pleasure. "More, touch me below."

He sank his hand under the water, caressed her clit and marked her yet again with his teeth, this time lower, at the base of her throat and as he did, she reached down and grasped his cock, her fingers firm as she worked him in long pulls.

"No, Bella. I'm too close to coming." He should pull away, only he couldn't and instead pushed deeper into her exquisite touch.

"So am I. My hand is going to bring forth your pleasure this time, not your own as you did on the ledge." She made a breathy sound that broke him and with his need so painful, he allowed her touch and when she cried so breathily against his lips, he plunged one finger inside her slick heat and indulged himself in the silken tightness of her body as she careened over the edge. As she did, he came hard on the heels of her, his mouth on hers as he gave her his pleasure right back in return.

"Now I'll shift," she murmured against his lips as she came

back down from where she'd transcended to. "Shift with me."

Sparks flared from her and he held her tight as she became all soft fur and nuzzling muzzle. She pushed her snout into his neck, her bear all claws as she clung to him and giving her no further warning, he dove with his sweet little bear into the welcoming warmth of the water.

* * * *

Hot water flowed over Bella's head as her bear sank into the pool with Jamie's arms wrapped snugly around her. This cave would always be theirs, a sacred place where they'd finally given each other what the other had needed, although unfortunately she was missing one crucial element—a full joining and along with it, the merged link of the mind. She wanted it all with him, desperately wanted it, only she also understood why they must wait.

As Jamie surfaced with her near the water's edge where it lapped onto the sand, he shifted, bright lights glimmering all around and his big bear getting all fiercely pushy as he nudged her bear from the water up onto the beach. He butted her backside with his snout until she padded out.

She plodded along the sandy curve of the pool rimmed with boulders and shook her body. Water sprayed from the thick matting of her golden fur and Jamie lumbered in beside her, lifted up onto his hind legs and toppled her over.

She rolled in the sand, him playfully coming down over top of her, his tongue lolling out and swiping across her chin.

In a blaze, he shifted again and flopped onto his back beside her.

She curled into him, dropped one paw onto his wide chest and nipped his neck with her bear's sharp teeth.

"Do you want to take another bite out of me too?" Chuckling, he rolled toward her, cupped her furry face in his hands and touched his nose to her muzzle.

Boy did she ever, but she'd behave for now. So relaxed and

satisfied from their lovemaking, she closed her eyes and let her bear snuggle deeper into Jamie's hold. She dozed as he petted her, his big hands stroking her back and sides. This was heaven, absolute heaven.

"Are you hungry, Bella?"

Famished. She'd missed lunch even though she'd packed it in her backpack, and with the moon high, dinner now as well.

"I can scent honey sandwiches in your bag, and I brought some things myself. Let me get dressed and I'll lay it all out." He shoved to his feet, belted his kilt at his waist and left his chest bare. From within her backpack, he flapped out her tartan blanket and seated on it, removed the sandwiches, apple and water bottle she'd packed inside earlier, then flipping the flap back on his own satchel, added his own offerings to the mix, a butter chicken wrap oozing with rice and sliced carrot, and a container he pulled the lid off which held cheese tortellini, bacon and crunchy broccoli. He dropped a fork into the pasta dish then removed another container and lifted the lid. The spectacular chocolate and raspberry split cheesecake inside had her making the Change.

Honey sandwiches be gone. She wanted what he'd brought.

"How'd you have time to pack all this?" With her hair lying damply down her back, she crawled toward him.

"I grabbed a meal from the kitchens. It was already all packaged." He held up a hand and she halted her crawl. With his other hand, he pulled out a red silk bra and matching panties from his sporran, the same lingerie she'd pegged on the line that morning.

"You stole my underwear?" Her words came out far too husky.

"Apparently I now have a fetish for them. Don these, otherwise this food will all go to waste and you'll be the main meal instead. My main meal."

Well, she had no issue with being his main meal, but since

her belly rumbled and the sight of the food had her mouth watering, she wouldn't mind some actual sustenance first so she had all the energy she needed to make love with him for what remained of the rest of the night.

She caught her underwear as he lobbed them to her, donned them then slipped into the clothing she'd bundled near the boulder, her short white summer shirt and matching cropped top. Jamie watched her dress with avid fascination, and grinning, she tossed him his shirt. "You need to wear a little more too, otherwise dinner will be a very short affair."

"Will do." He pulled the loose white cotton over his head and patted the space on the tartan beside him. "Come here. I wish to serve you."

"That sounds promising." She dropped down next to him. "Where are we starting with this delicious meal?"

"The butter chicken." Leaning forward, he picked up the wrap and held it to her mouth.

"Thank you." She bit into it, and the rich and buttery flavors danced on her tongue.

He took a bite as well, then offered her a forkful of cheesy tortellini pasta.

The moonlight streaming through the cavity in the craggy ceiling above, danced across his dark hair and lit the damp ends a golden hue, which matched his golden shifter eyes to perfection. "We'll have to return home in the morning." She sipped from her water bottle then offered the drink to Jamie. "Isla will be waiting for me at the cabin just after dawn. Did you drive to the cabin, or find it as you trekked?"

"I drove to the cabin then trekked here once I caught your scent." He touched the marks he'd made either side of her neck, his thumb gently swirling over them. "This night, I give you my vow, Bella. I will honor your needs above my own. All that I am is yours, my love, my steadfast commitment, and my unending devotion. There is only you…forever you."

"I was trying to move the subject away from us so that we might finish this meal before I demanded more playtime, but since you've now gone and sabotaged that idea"—she caught his face between her hands and kissed him, whispered against his lips—"don't ever leave me again, Jamie Matheson."

"Does this mean we're dating?" Playfully, he nipped her lower lip.

"Only if you agree to sharing your dessert."

"It's all yours." He picked up the cheesecake, dipped a spoon into it and slid the sweet confection between her lips.

The rich chocolate collided with the tart berries and she moaned her approval, then did so a second time as he captured her mouth with his and licked across her tongue. "You sure know how to feed a girl, my bossy bear."

"We'll finish the rest of this off later. I promise you we shall, although right now this bossy bear doesn't care to see you in clothes. It was wrong of me to ask you to dress." He set the dessert aside, tipped her back onto the tartan and with his eyes all passion-bright and sparking with wonder, he played with her so beautifully.

Chapter 11

The next morning Bella dressed in the clothes Jamie had pilfered from the line and folded into his bag, a bright red and white striped skirt and red tank top, then with even more marks already gracing her already marked neck, she smiled at him as they left their underground cavern and tramped back to the cabin.

Alongside the river, Jamie kept pace two steps behind her, his cheery whistle lightening her heart. Giggling, she wriggled her bottom at him then screeched as he caught her up and tossed her over his shoulder.

"Jamie!" Her belly thumped into his rock hard shoulder, her hair flinging into her face. She pushed the golden veil out of her eyes and sighed at his equally rock hard buttocks moving with his steady gait right at her eye-level. Grinning, she caressed his backside, the black leather of the pants he'd dressed in this morning molding each fine cheek.

"Aye," he murmured, his voice so husky and rough as he slipped one hand under her skirt hem and along the insides of her legs. That spot was slightly sore, abraded by his stubble, and made so by the interesting ways in which he'd staked his possession of her once again this morning before they'd left their sacred place. Even now, she wanted his mouth on her, and in all the same places once more.

"One second." She heaved up, managed to swing back over then slithered into his arms as he caught her. "You ready for what's to come?"

"As ready as I'll ever be." He popped a kiss on the tip of her nose. "Tonight's the night that counts."

"Bella Matheson!" Isla stormed through the trees glaring like a mad woman, then narrowed that glare even further on her neck before switching it to Jamie's neck. "Please tell me you didn't attempt to claim Bella before the full moon, Jamie."

"There was no attempt. I claimed every single fine inch of her, although we didn't join as one if that's what you're asking. That I'm leaving for tonight when the full moon rises." Jamie lowered her to her feet and stepped up to Isla. "We're returning to the keep now and when we do, we'd like to have you on our side. Surely you can see we're soul bound."

"Being mated myself, I can't deny you two have something amazing going on, but only the night of the full moon will really bring about the truth." Isla squeezed his shoulder. "Not much longer now."

"Not much longer indeed." She slipped past Jamie and Isla and continued on alongside the river toward the cabin. Tonight couldn't come soon enough now for her liking. She couldn't be more certain that Jamie was hers, particularly after last night.

The crunch and rustling of footsteps behind her gave proof Jamie and Isla both followed, and she picked up her pace. Before too long, she emerged from the woods and jogged across the clearing. She hiked it up the front step, snuck the key out from under the earthenware pot and unlocked the chunky wooden door.

She'd miss this cozy cabin she'd called home this past month. She drifted around the kitchen and checked all the appliances were turned off, that the slate-gray benches were cleaned and the rubbish bag removed from under the sink. She tied it off and left it by the front door where Isla and Jamie waited, both quietly conversing. No arguments thankfully. They chatted about his time away going lone bear and where he'd gone. She'd caught up with that during the night, so she left them to it and packed her bag in the bedroom, tidied the bunk with its golden-quilted cover and gave the bathroom a quick clean.

"Got everything?" Jamie stood leaning against the doorway watching her, his loose white shirt with its low V neck allowing the full exposure of the marks she'd given him this past night to show. With his belted sword glinting in the sunshine streaming through the netted window, he looked every lip-smacking inch the fierce Highland warrior he was.

"Almost." She sashayed up to him, ran her hands through his hair and fixed his messy dark locks. Touch. It was so important to their shifter kind, and particularly between mates.

"Isla and I messaged the chief while you were in here and updated him. He wants to talk to us both on our return." He leaned in and nuzzled her neck, embedding more of his scent into her.

"What did you tell him?"

"That it'll rip my heart out if a bond doesn't form between us tonight." Still nuzzling and with a swish of his fingers, he lifted her bag from the bunk bed and floated it over, then with a low growl, he sank his teeth into the most sensitive spot where her shoulder and neck met.

She arched into him, managed to snag her bag out of the air as it wobbled from his loss of control, then gasped as he bent her back half over, tugged her tank top down and bit into the upper swell of her breasts. A heavy level of frustration and need pounded into her, all coming from him and she waited as he continued to nip and bite her skin until those emotions slowly dispersed.

"Feeling better now?" She stroked her fingers through his

hair.

"We're about to head into battle, and with our own kin no less. I'll feel better once we've fully completed the bond, and not a minute earlier."

"I promise not to let anyone hurt you when we return. I'm the one who allowed your touch, and I'll make sure they're all made aware of that."

He chuckled, nipped her lips this time and chuckled some more. "Stop making me laugh. I hardly need you keeping the other males from hurting me. Telekinesis, remember? I can lift and swing them any which way I want."

"I know you can, but this thing between us is big and I need them to know that too."

"It's bigger than big. These visions, the ones we've jointly had, have set a ton of strange thoughts plaguing me. I got the distinct understanding from Jamie in the past that he went into battle before he and Annabella could speak vows, and in doing so, lost the chance he'd desired in which to join with her and complete their bond."

"You said it was your fault we've spent centuries apart." She'd never forget those strange words he'd uttered yesterday before she'd hung up on him, yet never had such strange words ever rung with such absolute truth as well.

"I've no idea why I said that, only that it felt completely right coming from my mouth. Let's get back home and talk to the chief." He set her back on her feet, scooped up her bag and catching her hand, guided her from the room.

Outside, she locked the cabin and slid the key back under the pot, while Jamie stowed her case in the trunk of Isla's SUV, his own gleaming black SUV parked on the other side of the clearing. Opening the passenger door, he gestured her in.

"You don't want to ride with us? We can come back tomorrow and collect your vehicle."

"Better to play it safe and have you ride with Isla. You'll

distract me into making a pit-stop otherwise, one which will see me nibbling on every single inch of you. I'll be right behind you."

"Argh, I so want the nibbling." Still, she climbed in and sat in the front seat while Isla took the driver's side, the rise of her belly brushing the wheel. Her dearest friend pulled out and she released a long breath as they left the calm and tranquility of the cabin behind. This place had been a refuge for her soul, and now since Jamie's arrival, even more so. High above, the odd streak of white cloud cut into the vivid blue sky and two sparrows chirped and landed on the spiky branch of a pine tree swaying beside the river. White water cascaded over thick boulders and flowed downstream, the grass growing lusher where it butted up to the stony riverbank, while a spray of wildflowers slashed the vivid green with their abundance of bright colors.

Jamie pulled in behind them as they bumped down the dirt trail, the brush and brambles growing wild in the center strip and either side of the thin track. The scrub scraped the undercarriage and the sides of the SUV, while heavy boughs of leafy elm and oak cascaded over their roof and gave the sense of them driving through a tunnel of dense greenery. Fifteen minutes later, they turned onto the washed-out side road and she flicked on the player and tried to relax as her favorite music wafted from the speakers.

"How are you feeling right now?" Isla reached across and squeezed her arm.

"Elated, yet also scared. I want the bond with Jamie, and only with him."

"I'll never forget standing in the inner courtyard when I awaited the bond to form with one of our own unmated males. I was elated, yet scared too. Then devastated when so many of our clansmen held such hope and I'd dashed it all by being the one to be mated to a shifter outside of our clan."

"It's not your fault your mate belongs to Gilleoin's other

shifter line.”

"Almost every one of the unmated men told me the same thing the next day. They even understood why I chose to run from Iain for the first five years following each full moon. I'm not running from him anymore though." With a soft smile, she stroked her belly where her twin sons lay. "I can't wait for these two to arrive."

"I can't wait to meet them—" Images tickled the periphery of her mind and she gasped.

"What is it?" Another squeeze of her arm from Isla.

"It's a vision." She closed her eyes as the motor hummed and they bounced along. The dark of the night surrounded her as she stood on the battlements in a corner where the guards rarely patrolled, her white fur cloak tied tightly around her neck and a heavy mist shrouding her. Grief pummeled her. Jamie had perished earlier that morn, passing from a head and neck wound which hadn't stopped bleeding from the battle he'd fought in. Now, she desired her own death too. Nay, she shook her head. The other Annabella desired her death, only it was as if they shared the same body, their emotions tangled and so very closely entwined together. No more did she stand as a witness to what was going on—she was Annabella. She braced her hands either side of the crenellation before her and climbed atop it. The wind rushed at her and on the stony edge she wobbled, her hands raised to the heavens above and tears streaking down her cheeks. Her thoughts returned to the precious time she and Jamie had spent together in the cavern a week past. He still hadn't kissed her that day, but he had promised he would when they sealed their vows. That cavern would always remain their sacred place and sobbing, all she wished to do was cease her pain and join him. Aye, Nessa had told Jamie that she'd *seen* he would be reborn in the twenty-first century, and Jamie had told Nessa to tell her to meet him there. Wherever he led, she would follow.

She tottered, the jagged rocks below soon to be her

deathbed. No more pain. It would soon all be gone. This was what she wanted, what she—

"Bella." Isla shook her shoulder hard and she lurched back.

Her vision cleared, although not the emotions. Those continued to roar through her, as if the connection still remained in place between her and the other Annabella.

"Are you all right? Speak to me."

"Jamie's dead." Tears flowed down her cheeks, her grief for the other Annabella's lost mate gripping her hard. "I had another vision and this time I no longer stood as a witness to what was happening, but rather it was as if I was as one with Annabella. She intended on jumping from Matheson Castle's ramparts."

"Perhaps your visions are so strongly connected with this other Annabella's emotions because you're an empath."

"She's an empath too, and she can't possibly live with the grief still consuming her. They never had a chance to complete their bond. Her Jamie still hadn't even kissed her. They were to seal their vows soon, but his death came first, and those thoughts I caught easily." Such confusion stormed through her. "Why am I seeing what I'm seeing?"

"We're almost home. You need to talk to the chief and see what he's got to say about all of this." Isla negotiated a tight turn in the track, and up ahead, the fortified walls of Matheson Castle rose sure and strong.

The blue-green waters of Loch Alsh washed in against the pebbly shoreline, the waves rocking the boats moored at the sea-gate, while there on the ramparts near the far corner facing away from the loch, jagged boulders rose, the very spot where the other Annabella had teetered on the edge before seeking her death. Just as well she hadn't seen her jump in her vision. She shuddered as Isla parked the vehicle in the large lot at the rear, one filled with their clan's dark SUVs. Aye, it was most definitely time to talk to Murdock and find out what these visions were about. They had to mean something.

She released her seatbelt, jumped out, jogged across to the postern gate and dashed inside.

Along the battlements in a dark shirt and pants with his sword belted at his side, Liam lifted a hand and waved. She waved back but kept running, right past a dozen of her kinsmen, who shirtless and in their belted kilts, trained hard with their swords in hand.

Hunter stepped out from amongst them, caught her up as she streaked past and swung her into his arms in a bone-crushingly tight hold. "It's about damn time you got home." He gently set her down on her feet and gripping her shoulders, searched her gaze. "What's wrong? Why are you running as if the very hounds of hell are on your tail?"

"I have to find the chief. I'm not sure what's wrong, but I've had three visions, all involving a woman who looks just like me, who also holds my name. She's mated to a man who looks just like Jamie and holds his name, and they both lived in ancient times. She's an empath, and he's a telekinetic. The similarities between the four of us are too striking for this not to mean something, and I feel as if I'm meant to help her. I also feel as if I'm running out of time to do whatever it is I'm supposed to do for her. She's about to end her life."

"You've connected somehow to a woman from the past? Through your empath skill?"

"Aye, but there's more to it than that. So much more."

"Bella!" Jamie tore across the inner courtyard, dust flying as he ran and one snarling rumble tearing from deep within him. He swished his fingers and Hunter rose, flipped over in midair and with his head dangling six feet from the ground, Jamie bounded in beside her. "Isla said you had another vision."

"Aye, Jamie is dead and the other Annabella wishes to end her life." She motioned to the ramparts near the far corner. "That's where she chooses to see to the task."

"Let's get to Murdock now."

"Hello?" Frowning something wicked, Hunter flicked his fingers at Jamie. "What's with tossing me upside down, eh?"

"I thought is best considering the news you're about to learn." Jamie grasped Hunter's swaying shoulder. "I've always considered you like my brother, even though you're not."

"As I have with you." Hunter's gaze narrowed on Jamie's neck and the marks she'd put there. He gritted his teeth and muttered, "Are those from my little sister?"

"Aye, and right now I need to look after her first. She's not the only one to have had visions from the past. What she's seen, I've seen, except for her last vision."

"Bella! Jamie!" Hands resting on his second floor window, Murdock leaned out the window of his solar and bellowed, "Inside, and make it quick. Both of you."

"I'm coming." She popped a kiss on Hunter's dangling forehead, snagged Jamie's arm and raced inside. Taking the stairs two at a time, she bounded upstairs with Jamie right beside her and together, they skidded into the chief's private sanctum.

In navy pants and a leather belt, his white button-down shirt rolled to his elbows, Murdock perched on the stone sill while the ancient elm tree outside swayed in the brisk breeze and its branches scraped against the thick stone walls of the keep. "I understand you two have questions. Nessa, the seer of ancient times, had a vision some time ago, one I wasn't permitted to speak to you about. You two have been able to connect so strongly of late because your souls are entwined with those of Annabella and Jamie's from the past. In fact, you two are Annabella and Jamie, their souls reborn here in the twenty-first century."

Such a wave of empathy swelled out from Murdock as he walked across to her. Taking her hands in his, he continued, "I've been unable to intervene until this moment for fear I'd alter the natural course of your future, although now is the very time I can finally speak to you both about it. I've *seen* that that is so. In the past, a far greater future awaited both Jamie and Annabella here in this time, but in ancient times, they unfortunately never had the chance to complete their bond."

"How is it we've seen their memories from that time?"

"Those who go through rebirth usually don't recall their pasts, although you two seem to be the exception to the rule. I also believe in order for everything to come full circle for you both, before the full moon rises tonight, all must be made right."

"Are you saying we need to find our way back to the past?"

"That's exactly what I'm saying. Annabella from the past has always wished to complete her bond with Jamie, and deep in your soul, you've wished for it too." He cupped her cheek. "Do you understand what I mean?"

"Aye, I need to right the wrongs of Annabella and Jamie's pasts."

"Exactly." He eyed Jamie. "Jamie's spirit from the past has been calling out to you as well, and you need to return to the year twelve-hundred and eleven and aid him in making Annabella his. Make him set his stubborn pride aside and take her. Only then will the two of you both be able to set them fully free so you might live here in the future. If you don't, I've *seen* your visions will only worsen."

"I agree, Murdock." Whispered words from within the air itself, then the wind whistled all around their chief's solar, blowing papers from his chunky desk and scattering them all about. The pictures rattled on the walls and the floor shook under their feet, then a woman in a gown of cream and gold silk, one with long lacy sleeves that fluttered to her fingertips, appeared out of the rushing wind and took form before them. With her sparkly skin catching the sunlight through Murdock's window, she could be no other than their fae princess, the guardian of their Earthbound kind. The woman dipped her head toward her and smiled. "'Tis wonderful to see you again, Annabella."

"Bella." Her throat dried completely out, her name barely a

rasp between her lips. "I can't believe you're here." She'd never met the fae princess before, but she'd certainly heard of the legend surrounding her, as well as how Cherub had aided Isla in joining with Iain.

"Aye, Bella it is. My apologies, and I am here now because it's time for you to honor Annabella's wishes from the past. Her spirit calls out to you from across the ages, just as Jamie's spirit has called out to him. Neither of them can truly be at peace until you both return to the past and ensure all is made right. When Annabella jumped from the ramparts, I caught her. I aided her in her ascension beyond the veil, and due to that she never truly passed in the way that our people usually do. You're to make sure Annabella and Jamie complete their bond. That is what Annabella has always wanted." Grinning, Cherub caught her hand and twirled them both around, then snagged Jamie's hand within the swirling twist of wind. "I'm certain you two shall have fun seeing to this task, which means you need to hold on tight, both of you. This will be a bit of a bumpy ride since I cannae remain with you the entire way."

Oh goodness. Bella clutched ahold of Cherub tighter, the air all around them churning so violently.

"Don't fight the pull either," Murdock yelled over the blast, his hands cupped around his mouth.

The wind lashed at her and she fell away into a dark abyss. A blaze of stars shimmered, so bright and beautiful, the endlessness of time and space enveloping all three of them.

"Close your eyes," Cherub instructed. "Allow a full joining of souls when you arrive. 'Tis time for you both to live and breathe again, in the year twelve-hundred and eleven."

"I'll try." Fear and awe washed through her.

More images swirled.

Sitting on the ledge of their pool in his wet tunic, Jamie from ancient times watched Annabella as she floated with a hungry gaze. She suddenly jolted down, went under and almost took in a mouthful of water.

She tried to heave back up, then Jamie was there, his hands on her hips. He kicked and pushed them both upward and they broke the surface.

Shaking his head, drops flew from him and wet her.

"Jamie?" She searched his gaze, her fingers within the fingers of Annabella from the past. "We're really here. Are you all right?"

"I'm fine, and currently cohabitating this body with the other Jamie. I can sense him deep within me." He glanced toward the craggy ceiling where the golden orb of the full moon beamed. The cavern was dark, only lit by a trace of moonlight shimmering through. Slowly, he turned his gaze back on her and smiled so wickedly. "In traveling back to the past, it appears we've arrived on the night of a full moon."

She treaded water, the long skirts of her white shift tangling around her legs, while Jamie wore naught but a white tunic, his pants, boots and weapons gone. So was her red and white summer skirt and red tank top. The man before her also held a deep scar across his forehead. She touched the white line of what appeared to be an old injury. "When did you get hurt?"

He touched the scar himself, frowned then nodded. "The other Jamie said that happened some years ago, during a battle he fought alongside Gilleoin against the Chief of MacKenzie."

"Oh goodness. We're really here in their bodies, and they're with us." She went down again and he yanked her up. Spluttering, she rubbed water from her eyes. "Ah, I'm feeling rather waterlogged. Do you mind if we swim to the ledge?"

"Of course not. Come." He kicked them toward it and once they came up alongside the ledge, he lifted her from the water and sat her on the edge then with his hands either side of her legs, hoisted himself up and toppled her backward.

"Jamie, what are you doing?"

He leaned closer, touched his forehead to hers, and rasped,

"Have you forgotten what Murdock and Cherub told us must happen?"

"No, I haven't." Now she was here it was time for her to honor Annabella's wishes from the past. It was time to complete her bond with Jamie and ensure all was made right, and now she had Jamie close again, she wrapped her legs around the back of his legs, his heavenly weight nestled so deliciously on top of her. "Kiss me." The other Annabella pushed forward with giddy hope. She wanted Jamie's kiss so badly. "Make it a really good one too. The other Annabella has been looking forward to this for what feels like centuries."

"As you wish, my sweet little Bella."

Ever so gently, he pressed his lips against hers, and the moment he did, deep inside her the other Annabella clutched ahold of him while she settled deeper within her ancestor to allow her this moment. The other Annabella cupped Jamie's cheeks in her hands, her next words so hopeful. "I have something to tell you, Jamie, but the other Jamie. Bring him forth."

Jamie closed his golden shifter eyes and when he opened them again, they blazed a solid brown instead. "I'm here, my love."

"In a week's time, you'll pass away from a head and neck wound you'll suffer in a battle with the MacKenzie and we'll miss our wedding day which is to come a week following that, although I've kept my word to you. Wherever you have lead us, I have followed, all the way to the twenty-first century. I am now merged with the woman who I shall be in the future, her thoughts now my thoughts, and I'm aware that although neither of us may change your coming death or my ascension beyond the veil, we've still been granted this one night to make amends. Dinnae turn me away again. We must make this time count." She pressed one hand against his chest through the wet cotton of his white tunic, the heavy beat of his heart beyond soothing and everything within both her and the other Annabella settled. Slowly, her ancestor reached between her and Jamie, lifted the hem of his tunic and even though his brow pulled down, she stripped it from him then curled her fingers around his heavy shaft and looking deep into his eyes, murmured, "Make us one. I want my chosen one, for us to never live upon this Earth without each other again. Reunite our souls, both from the present and the future."

"That I can do." Jamie jerked against her, his eyes closing then reopening a moment later, his irises gleaming a molten gold once more. "Bella?" He gave her a shake and she squeezed her eyes shut and opened them again. He smiled when she did. "You're back."

"I never went anywhere. The other Annabella wants this moment with the other Jamie, just as much as I want it with you. We are one and the same."

"Then from this day forth you'll be mine, just as I'll always be yours. May I undress you, my seductive siren?"

"I don't know why you haven't already. I've already stripped your shirt off." Well, the other Annabella had, and she'd encouraged her the entire time.

A chuckle as he rose to his feet and drew her up to stand beside him. He pushed her against the craggy rock wall with his body. "I love you so much, far beyond our own time, and all the way back again."

"I love you too, no matter what century that might be within."

"Perfect." He crouched, grasped her hem and lifted the cotton. Fabric in hand, he drew it up, past her knees then hips and over her head. He flapped it out and laid it down on the slick stone surface of the ledge. "Our bed is now ready."

"It surely—" She squealed as he swooped in, then he took her breath away as he captured her mouth and devoured her in a passionate kiss. Oh my, her Jamie certainly knew how to kiss and as he plunged his tongue into her mouth and cupped her breasts, she and the other Annabella sighed with delight.

"This feels so right." With her back against the wall, she lifted one leg, wrapped it around the back of his legs and tugged him ever closer. "This mated bond is so wonderful."

"And now it's about to be ours. The other Jamie is giving in fast, his stubborn pride disintegrating." He rubbed against her, his chest hair scraping over her puckered nipples and making them stiffen to hard points.

Such joy and happiness swarmed forth within her and she ran her fingertips over Jamie's wide chest and down along the rigid bands of his abs until tentatively, she wrapped her fingers around his massive erection which she wanted deep inside her. "Do you think we'll be able to forge the merged link of the mind like this, what with us being in the past now and not the future? Only shifters can forge the merged link and our ancestors weren't shifters, but instead of Nessa's fae blooded line alone."

"I want that merged link, and if I don't get it now, I'm going to get it the moment we return to the future." He weighed her breasts in his hands, eased them together and slowly licked one nipple.

The hot stroke of his tongue sent such delicious shivers racing through her body.

"You're so damn tasty, no matter what time either of us have lived within." He swirled around the other tip, sucked her nipple deep into his mouth until a torrent of tingles raced through her.

"I ache to join our bodies together as one. So does the other Jamie. He wants it bad, wished he'd never chosen to wait." He lifted his head, captured her mouth and kissed her again, with such ravenous intent and she fondled the head of his cock, stroked down his shaft and speared her fingers into the lush dark curls at the apex of his groin.

"We should take this slow, so that our other selves might be able to truly enjoy this moment as well."

"I'll try, but I'm burning with a hunger right now that I'm struggling to contain." He pushed her harder into the ledge wall, skimmed his warm hands down her sides and over her hips before slowly lowering to his knees. Crouched before her, he caressed her inner thighs, his breath puffing hotly against her most sensitive flesh. Then he breathed deep, his gaze zeroing in on her lower entrance. Gently, he parted her folds and let out a ragged groan. "I'm going to give you two seconds to tell the other Annabella what I'm about to do. It's time to right the wrongs of our past, for me to taste every exquisite inch of you, then to complete the bond and come together fully as one."

"I think she already knows what you're about to do." And the other Annabella itched inside of her for more as well. "She wants you to hurry it along."

"It appears you've never changed, not in all these centuries." Chuckling, he glided his fingers along her lower entrance, slipped one finger inside her then carefully added a second and glancing up at her as he pushed deeper inside, smiled so wickedly. "Do you trust me?"

"Always, no matter what century that might be within."

"Good answer." He stroked deeper, suctioned his mouth over her nub and sucked, hard.

She cried out as intense pleasure slammed through her, and her ancestor swayed and cried out for even more, her thoughts clear to read. "Don't stop. We both love this attention."

"As you wish." Head bent, he spread her legs even wider and licked her deeper, every flick of his tongue over her clit sending such exquisite heat roaring through her. He suckled and her core pulsed and shattered as wave after wave of pure bliss rocked through her.

She came, so swift and fast and he scooped her up before she fell, laid her down on her discarded shift, his mind battering against hers and demanding entrance as in the way of soul bound shifter mates.

She and her ancestor both opened their mind fully to him. "Never will I accept another, other than you." She hooked her legs around his legs, and he gripped her hips and slowly, carefully, skimmed his cock along her slick folds.

He nudged, right at her entrance.

"Do it, Jamie." She cupped his tight buttocks and rocked underneath him, pulled him ever closer and he thrust, tore through her thin barrier below and as he did, his mind barreled into hers with a force that stated his claim, that he'd never relinquish her again. Together, he'd joined them in all ways, their minds and bodies, their hearts and souls, their past and their future. Forever they'd remain interlocked, across the ages and until the very end of time.

Aye, never had she given herself so fully or freely before, and as her chosen one's mind tunneled ever deeper inside hers, she rose up to meet the private pathway he'd created between them and snapped the bond firmly into place. With that final link cemented, she whispered into his mind, *"You're now exactly where you belong. You're my bossy bear, my lover, the other half of my very soul."*

"As you're the other half of my soul. Where I go, you go, no matter what time that might be within."

"Aye, you can guarantee I'll follow your every step." She stretched out underneath him, the initial pain of this new joining subsiding, and her soul so filled with exhilaration. *"I feel so incredibly full."*

"I've never felt so whole, as if my search for you has crossed the centuries and now finally met completion." Ever so gently, he eased back out then as the tip of his cock brushed her sensitive clit, he pushed all the way back in again with a feral moan. *"I want to bring you untold pleasure. Keep your mind open to mine so I can sense what you're feeling, so I can share all of my thoughts as well."*

"*Always.*" Clinging to him, her arms wrapped tightly around his neck and her legs firm around his hips, she greedily accepted all of him, the pain of earlier having fully eased as Jamie's desire for more swamped her. "*I love you.*"

"*I love you too, my sweet little Bella.*" He thrust deeper, slowly but surely then he pounded hard and as he did, he caught the skin of her neck between his lips and nipped.

"*Are you going to bite me?*"

"*Hell, yes, and every single day to come.*" One very territorial rumble escaped his throat. "*Bite me as well, Bella. I need your claiming mark in this time as well.*"

"*You'll have it.*" Of her body's own accord, she rocked underneath him and as he scraped his teeth over the fiercely beating pulse point in her neck, she did the same with him then when she could no longer hold on, she bit down and marked him, hard. He was her mate, her lover, the other half of her very soul.

"*Do that again,*" he growled as he lunged into her, over and over, his pace so fiercely frantic.

Bucking under him, her soul fully entwined with his and her love for him soaring free, she reveled in their absolute joining, then bit down and marked him again.

He roared, sank his teeth into her neck and sent her careening heavenward, her thoughts and the other Annabella's both flying.

Together, they cried out his name, his mark pure possession and exactly what they needed, this joining one they'd forever crave, until the very end of time.

* * * *

With his cock buried deep within Bella's hot channel, Jamie held perfectly still as her pleasure wrapped itself around him. Deep within him, more pleasure swarmed through from his kindred spirit from centuries past. His other half had reveled in the moment of joining with their chosen one and making her his, wanted to do so again, over and over and to never stop.

Of that, they'd always be in agreement.

Hell, he could certainly drown in the current satisfied smile lifting his woman's lips, wanted only to—he jerked backward.

The wind whipped all around him and something pulled at his very soul and tore him fully free of his ancestor. The dark took him and sent him soaring through an endless array of blackness, the wide void the same which had first brought him here.

"Jamie!" Bella screamed, the sound wrenching at his heart.

"Where are you?"

"I'm here, and the other Annabella is gone. I've left her behind." Another cry and then she appeared within the churning abyss. Lightning sizzled and the wind shoved and twirled her about.

"I'm coming." He flattened his hands to his sides and head down, dove toward her. So close. He pitched to one side, flung out a hand and snatched her around the waist then tumbled as he tried to keep ahold of her.

"Don't let me go." She clung to him, her arms around his neck and her legs tangled with his as they leveled out. "This moving through time is both scary and amazing. I wonder where Cherub is?"

"I've no idea, but since she's the only one who can open a portal through time, then this is definitely all her doing." Bright lights blazed and twinkled all about.

"I got pulled away from Annabella so fast. I didn't have time to say goodbye to her." She shoved her blond hair out of her face and gazing into his eyes, once again sank into his mind. "*We still have our merged link.*"

"*And it feels incredible.*" He wouldn't be able to wipe the grin from his face for the rest of his life. Mated, fully and completely, and with the woman whom he'd loved for centuries upon centuries no less. "*No one will ever be able to tear us apart again.*"

"We're also without clothes." Her gaze lowered to his chest then farther down to his throbbing shaft. *"You're also clearly very happy about that."*

"Woman, don't expect me to be all floppy when you're rubbing yourself up against me in the nude." With her lush bottom in his hands, he lifted her up and brought her straight back down on top of his hungry cock, her hot folds a rush of heat encasing him from root to tip. He groaned, got a hell of a lot stiffer and when she rocked and took him even deeper, he dipped his head and molded his mouth to hers.

Kissing her, he plunged into her over and over again, going balls-deep in a manic rush.

"Oh my." She gasped, her eyelids fluttering shut and her hot channel squeezing him as pleasure rocked through her. It saturated him along their merged link and his balls tightened to the point of pain.

"You're mine," he whispered raggedly then bit down on the sensitive skin of her neck.

"As you're mine." She sucked on his neck, teeth razzing his skin. "I hope the other Annabella and Jamie are making love like this all over again."

"I do too. Mark me now, Bella. I need it."

"You belong to me, just as I belong to you." She bit down and he lost his vision. Everything exploded, bright lights flashing in all directions as he came, hard and fast.

In one hot rush, his seed spurted from him and coated her deep within, then as she rubbed her thumb over the mark she'd made on his neck, he slowly came back down and shook his head to clear it.

"Where'd you go, my bossy bear?" Her inner channel tightened so wickedly around him and she lapped the mark she'd made on his neck then inched a little farther along and bit him again, her heightened arousal still strong as it flew down their link and swamped him. "Have to—must come again."

"I've got you." He bit the other side of her neck and as she bucked into him, her channel contracted, pulsed over and over again and made him fly a second time, right to the heavens along with her.

"Jamie?" She licked his neck, right over the marks she'd given him. "Does it feel as if we're slowing down to you?"

A dark, dense fog swirled up ahead and they plunged through it, then an unearthly force sucked at them and they hit a soft mattress and bounced, sent the bedcovers flying all about them, then landed a second time before gently bouncing and fully settling.

He blinked and all came into full clarity. His desk sat in the corner, the door to his adjoining bathroom to the right, and his brown fur covers soft and warm under his back. The air swirled one final time and his weapons and clothes, as well as Bella's belongings *thunked* onto the ground beside his bed. "We're in my chamber, Matheson Castle. In the future thankfully."

"Well, the next time we see Cherub we'll need to thank her for dropping us back here and not anywhere else." Smiling wide, she caught a fluttering feather from his pillow and tickled it under his nose. "So, we've made love in a cavern, in another time, and in a portal. We may as well try and do this the normal way and see if this bed is any good. What do you say?"

"Making love to you anywhere sounds good to me." Laughing, he caught her face in his hands and kissed her, his chosen one a woman he'd follow to the ends of the Earth, no matter what century or time that might take him to.

Chapter 12

A few days later...

A bird's cheery chirp floated into the cavern from somewhere outside and Bella stirred awake on the sandy beach next to their sacred underground pool and curled more snugly into Jamie's arms. He lay on his back, his eyes open and the new day's rising sunshine filtering through the vent overhead and shimmering across the glassy surface of the hot water. Steam plumed and swirled all about, keeping them both toasty and warm.

With her cheek resting on his chest, she smiled and as he stroked her back, the urge to bite him again flashed through her. She grazed her teeth over his pec muscle then sank her teeth into him. Mmm, he was so tasty.

"Bella." He arched his back, his emotions flaring through to her as he reveled in her bite. Gritting his teeth, he demanded, "Harder."

She bit him again, deeper as he'd demanded then sighed with delight and sat up. With one leg slung over his hip, she straddled his thighs and giggled as his gaze got caught on her bobbing breasts. She scooped them together and leaned forward with the offering.

"You're reading my mind." He shoved his elbows underneath him, hoisted up and licked her nipples.

"I'm reading mine as well." Tapping his nose, she laughed. "You're insatiable, and I love it."

"Expect that to be the case for the next few centuries. I've waited a long time to finally know I've got an entire lifetime with you. I don't intend on wasting another minute of it. I also have a question for you." He caught her hand, pressed a kiss against her palm and with his stunning shifter eyes flaring an even brighter golden hue, murmured, "Please marry me, Annabella Matheson."

"Oh my, this is so sudden. You haven't changed your mind about speaking vows with me these past eight-hundred years?" She fluttered a hand over her chest. "You truly wish to wed?"

"Cease teasing me, woman." With a swish of his fingers, he lifted them both up, swept her in underneath him on the sand and with one powerful stroke, thrust deep, their bodies and souls completely entwined as one. "I love you, Bella."

"I love you too." She gasped at the sweet rightness of their joining. "And yes, I long to be your bride. You've got one week to make that happen."

"A perfect answer." Cupping the back of her head, he drew her mouth to his and kissing her, joined them together so wonderfully, just as she'd always desired.

He belonged to her, and now it was time to explore a new future, one that had always been destined to be theirs.

Precious love. It could cross the centuries, never to be extinguished, from this time to any other.

Author's Note

Clan Matheson descends from a twelfth century man called Gilleoin, a man who was believed to have been from the ancient Royal House of Lorne. The name Matheson has been attributed to the Gaelic words Mic Mhathghamhuim which means "Son of the Bear," and the clan chief's arms carry two bears as supporters. In the twelfth century, clan Matheson settled around the area of Loch Alsh, Loch Carron, and Kintail, and gave their allegiance to clan MacDonald whose chiefs were the Lords of the Isles. Clan Matheson became a large and powerful clan with a force of around two-thousand men, although by the middle of the sixteenth century they'd diminished greatly in size and influence due to the blood feuds raging across the isles at that time. This warring left them to possess less than a third of the original Matheson property on Loch Alsh.

It's time for the whispers to reignite. Clan Matheson are the "Son of the Bear."

This story is woven with as much accuracy to the period and locations as possible, although any mistakes made are mine alone. Please feel free to search for any of my other works. I simply adore strong heroines, and have a ton of fun matching them with their honorable alpha heroes.

Also available in paperback
Scottish Historical Romance

Traveling through time…for a Highlander.

Highlander Heat Series

Highlander's Castle, Book One

Highlander's Magic, Book Two

Highlander's Charm, Book Three

Highlander's Guardian, Book Four

Highlander's Faerie, Book Five

Highlander's Champion, Book Six

by Joanne Wadsworth

Looking for more sexy Scottish adventure?

Catch a teaser excerpt of the next book in
The Matheson Brothers series.

Highlander's Claim

The Matheson Brothers, Book Eleven

by Joanne Wadsworth

Highlander's Claim

The Matheson Brothers, Book Eleven

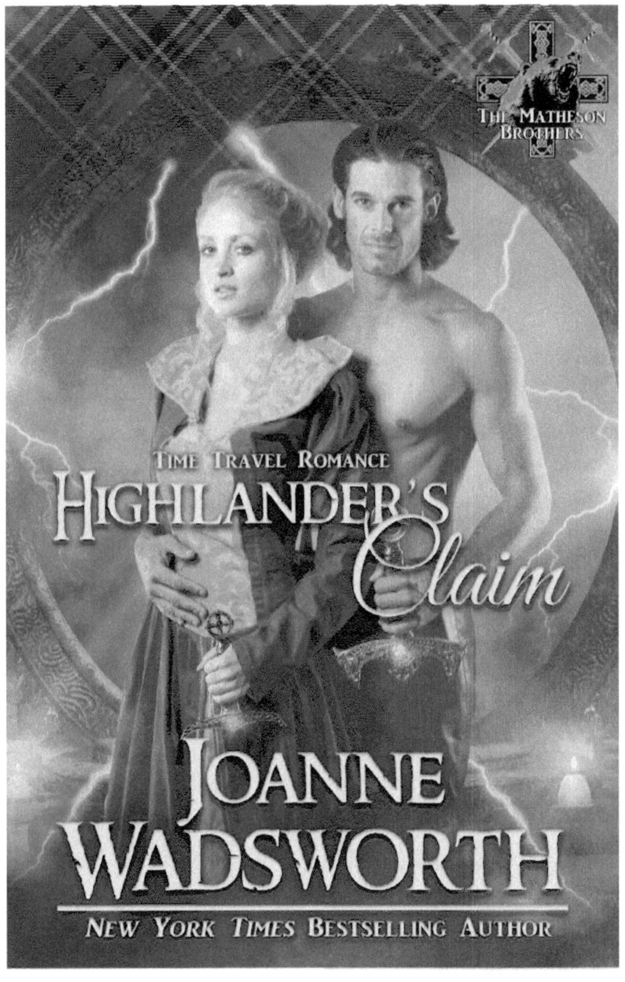

Teaser Excerpt

Ailith squeezed her hands into fists and tried not to open the door and bound back out. She both wanted to be with Hunter, and didn't. His safety was only assured if she set these rising emotions for him aside and returned to the past. She couldn't take him with her, and he wasn't permitted to follow. That was the only option moving forward, until she no longer saw a vision of him perishing.

The cracking of bones echoed under the door then the heavy thump and scratch of paws resounded. Shifters could be incredibly territorial and if they were mated, he would be even more territorial due to their bond. Somehow, he'd already tracked her down. Drat it all. She jiggled from foot to foot, so unsure as to what to do. Let Hunter come in and spell him to forget her again? Or ignore him?

More thumping and scratching, a bear's muzzle pressed to the gap under the doorway and a snort and growl rumbling through. Ugh, he wasn't leaving, not until she'd dealt with him again. Heart squeezing in on itself, she opened her door and leaned against the doorjamb, then tried her best to assert as much authority into her voice as she could. "What do you want?"

A big bear prowled back and forth, Hunter's clothing

scattered across the floor of the passageway. He'd shifted in a hurry, and boy, did she have her work cut out for her with him. His bear's golden shifter eyes drilled into hers, his beast holding a stunning brown pelt with white-tipped paws.

He rumbled another grizzly growl, then padded past her into her chamber before turning around in a slow circle in the middle of the room at the end of her four-poster bed. He sat on his rump on the white rug, his front legs straight and ears alert as he observed her like one did when examining a bug under a microscope. Aye, and she was currently the bug.

The Matheson Brothers

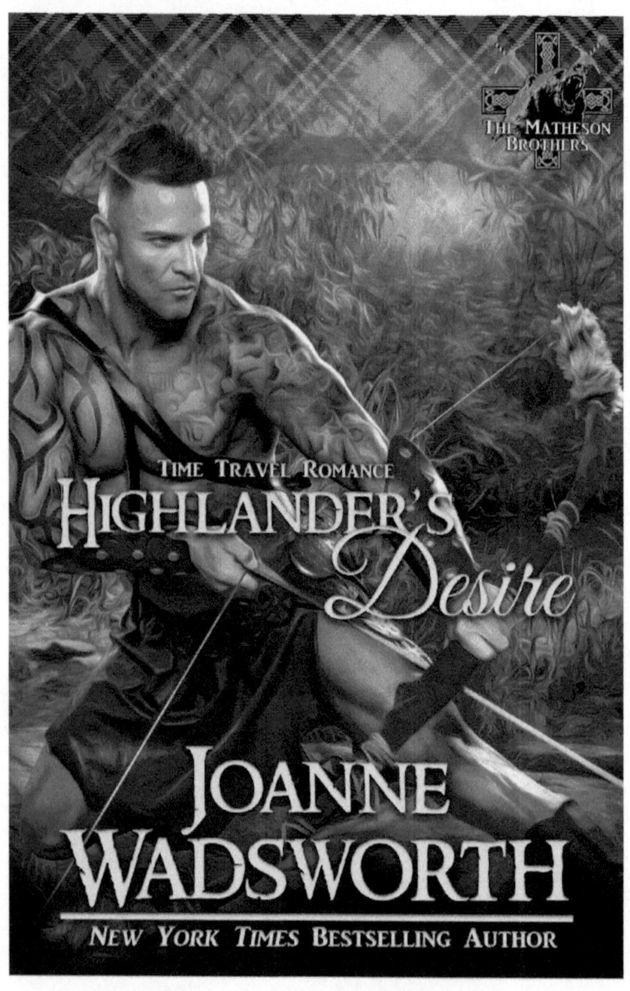

The Matheson Brothers Continued

Highlander's Kiss, Book Four
Highlander's Heart, Book Five
Highlander's Sword, Book Six

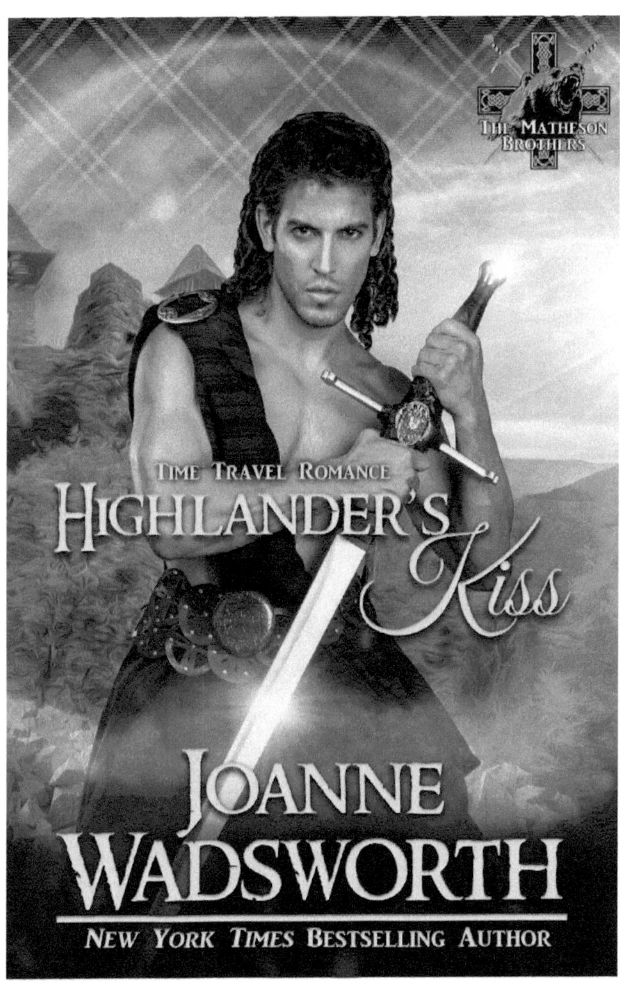

JOANNE WADSWORTH

The Matheson Brothers Continued

Highlander's Bride, Book Seven
Highlander's Caress, Book Eight
Highlander's Touch, Book Nine

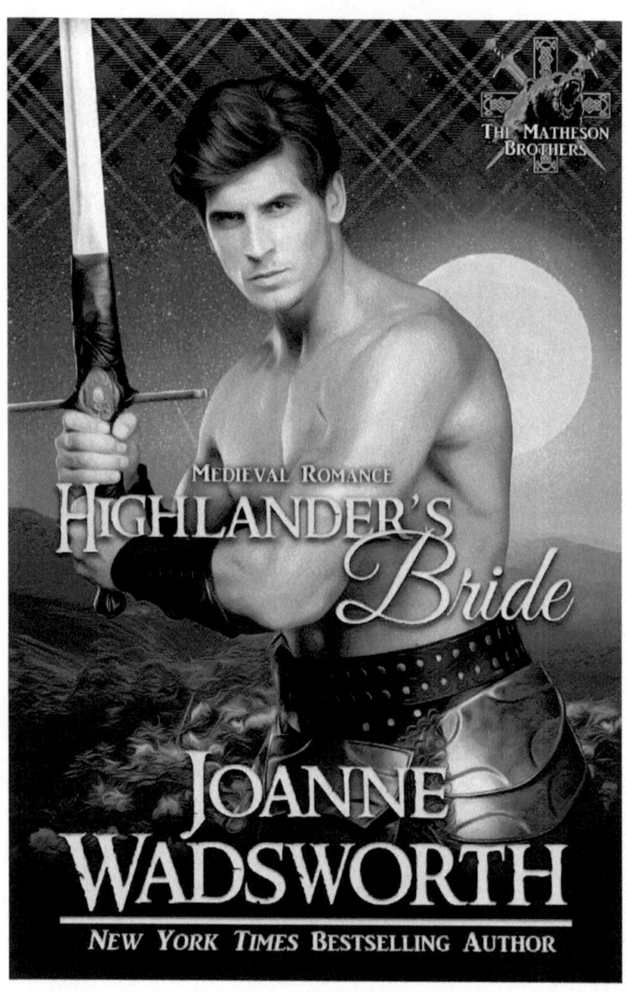

The Matheson Brothers Continued

Highlander's Shifter, Book Ten
Highlander's Claim, Book Eleven
Highlander's Courage, Book Twelve
Highlander's Mermaid, Book Thirteen

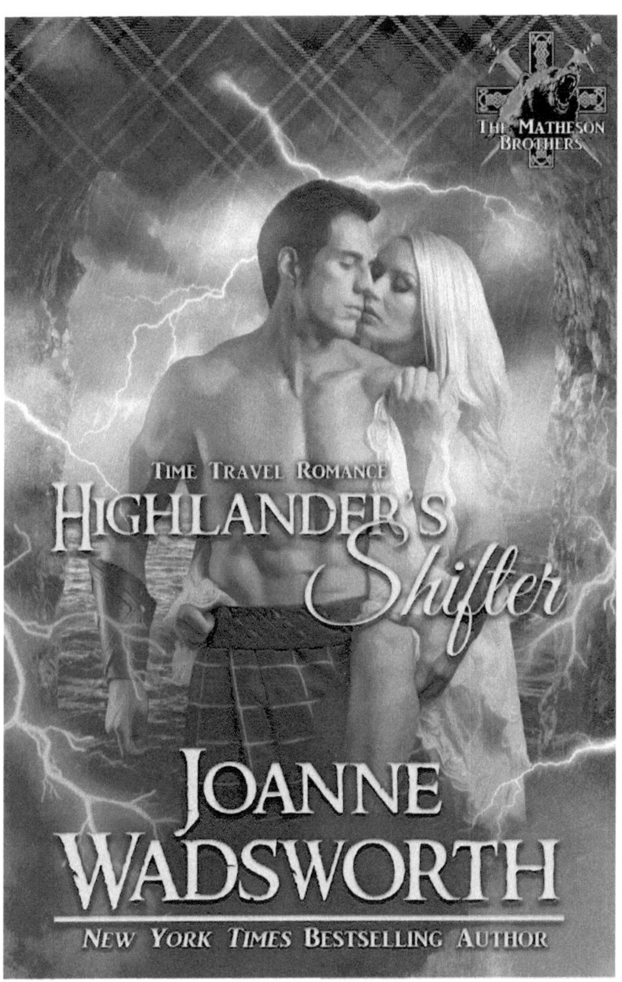

Highlander Heat

Highlander's Castle, Book One
Highlander's Magic, Book Two
Highlander's Charm, Book Three
Highlander's Guardian, Book Four
Highlander's Faerie, Book Five
Highlander's Champion, Book Six

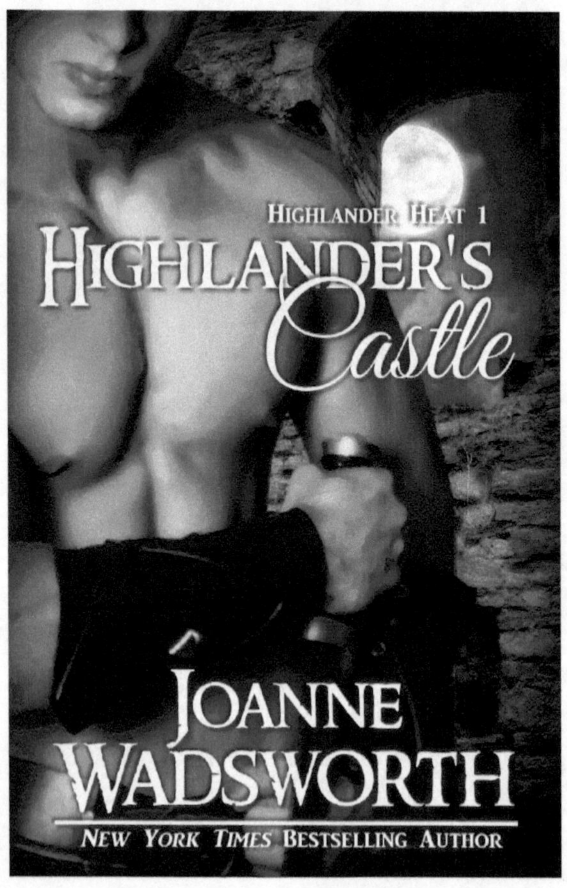

Regency Brides

The Duke's Bride, Book One
The Earl's Bride, Book Two
The Wartime Bride, Book Three
The Earl's Secret Bride, Book Four
The Prince's Bride, Book Five
Her Pirate Prince, Book Six

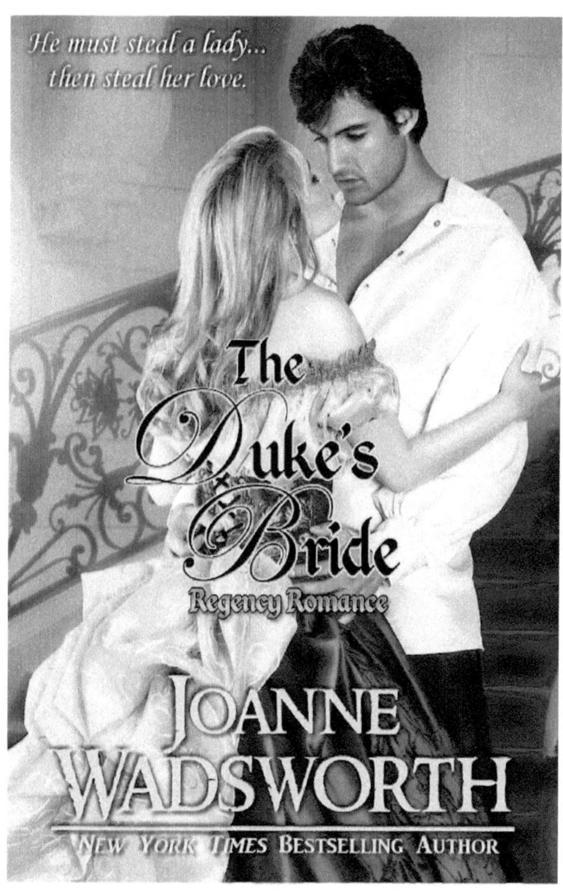

Princesses of Myth

Protector, Book One
Warrior, Book Two
Hunter (Short Story - Included in Warrior, Book Two)
Enchanter, Book Three
Healer, Book Four
Chaser, Book Five

Billionaire Bodyguards

Billionaire Bodyguard Attraction, Book One
Billionaire Bodyguard Boss, Book Two
Billionaire Bodyguard Fling, Book Three

JOANNE WADSWORTH

Joanne Wadsworth is a *New York Times* and *USA Today* Bestselling Author who adores getting lost in the world of romance, no matter what era in time that might be. Hot alpha Highlanders hound her, demanding their stories are told and she's devoted to ensuring they meet their match, whether that be with a feisty lass from the present or far in the past.

Living on a tiny island at the bottom of the world, she calls New Zealand home. Big-dreamer, hoarder of chocolate, and addicted to juicy watermelons since the age of five, she chases after her four energetic children and has her own hunky hubby on the side.

So come and join in all the fun, because this kiwi girl promises to give you her "Hot-Highlander" oath, to bring you a heart-pounding, sexy adventure from the moment you turn the first page. This is where romance meets fantasy and adventure…

To learn more about Joanne and her works, visit
http://www.joannewadsworth.com

www.ingramcontent.com/pod-product-compliance
Lightning Source LLC
Chambersburg PA
CBHW051228210726
48290CB00003B/860